A Coyote Ridge Christmas

The Walkers of Coyote Ridge, 7

Dead Heat Ranch

Boots Optional
Betting on Grace
Overnight Love

Devil's Bend

Chasing Dreams
Vanishing Dreams

Misplaced Halos

Protected in Darkness
Salvation in Darkness
Bound in Darkness

Office Intrigue

Office Intrigue
Intrigued Out of the Office
Their Rebellious Submissive
Their Famous Dominant
Their Ruthless Sadist
Their Naughty Student
Their Fairy Princess

Pier 70

Reckless
Fearless
Speechless
Harmless
Clueless

Sniper 1 Security

Wait for Morning
Never Say Never
Tomorrow's Too Late

Southern Boy Mafia/Devil's Playground

Beautifully Brutal
Without Regret
Beautifully Loyal
Without Restraint

STANDALONE NOVELS
Unhinged Trilogy
A Million Tiny Pieces
Inked on Paper
Bad Reputation
Bad Business

NAUGHTY HOLIDAY EDITIONS
2015
2016

A Coyote Ridge Christmas

THE WALKERS OF COYOTE RIDGE, 7

NICOLE EDWARDS

Published by Nicole Edwards Limited
PO Box 1086, Pflugerville, Texas 78691

A Coyote Ridge Christmas
The Walkers of Coyote Ridge, 7
Nicole Edwards

COVER DETAILS:
Image: © shsphotography (tree - 36622663) | 123rf.com
Image: © konstanttin (frame - 34032616) | 123rf.com
Design: © Nicole Edwards Limited

INTERIOR DETAILS:
Formatting: Nicole Edwards Limited
Editing: Blue Otter Editing | BlueOtterEditing.com

ISBN:
Ebook 9781644180105 | Paperback 9781644180112

SUBJECTS:
BISAC: FICTION / Romance / Contemporary
BISAC: FICTION / Romance / General

Dedication

Come back to Coyote Ridge for Christmas...

When Travis Walker finds himself uninspired about gifts for his family, he realizes what he wants to give them doesn't come wrapped in a box with a shiny bow on top.

This year, with the help of his brothers, Travis is going to pull off a surprise that'll lay the groundwork for the Walker Christmas tradition going forward.

Of course, Travis won't consider it a success unless he moves a few pieces on the proverbial chessboard while he's at it. As for where those will eventually land ... well, that's anyone's guess.

Chapter One

T MINUS FIFTEEN DAYS.

That was how much time Travis Walker had before Christmas was upon them, and as God was his witness, he had no idea what to get his ever-expanding family.

Not a fucking clue.

Which was the very reason he'd slipped out of work today, sneaking in a little private time to do some shopping. Here he was, three hours in, surrounded by hundreds of shoppers doing pretty much the same thing, and fuck-all, he was as empty-handed as he'd been when he started.

It should've been simple, really. Slip into a toy store, toss a few things in the cart for the kiddos, move on to the next store. Maybe a necklace for Kylie, a new wallet for Gage. Only, as he'd strolled through those stores, looked at those things, he hadn't been inspired. For whatever reason, he didn't think his wife, husband, and five precious kids would be impressed with all the material crap they could get for themselves.

Not that Travis had a clue what to do about that.

He paused to stare at the mall directory, hoping something would jump out at him.

"Well, I'll be damned."

He pivoted at the familiar voice, smiled when Sawyer came strolling toward him decked out in his regular attire of Wranglers, boots and the black felt Stetson he favored in winter. "What're you doin' here?"

Sawyer grinned. "Same thing you are, I suppose."

Travis held out his empty hands, showing his brother the proof of his failure. "Hope you've fared better than I have."

Sawyer mimicked his movement, hands empty. "Nope. And I've been at it since nine o'clock this mornin'."

Unable to help himself, Travis laughed. "You got me there. I've only been at it since lunch. We're a pair, aren't we?"

"That we are," Sawyer agreed. "Though a pair of what, I'm not sure."

Turning to survey the shoppers moving through the mall, he motioned Sawyer toward the Starbucks. "While we wait for inspiration to hit, let me buy you some coffee."

"I'd need somethin' far stronger for inspiration. But coffee'll do for now." Sawyer fell into step with him. "Does Gage know you're here?"

"No one knows," he admitted as they pulled up the rear of the Starbucks line, a good ten people deep. "And it looks as though I've wasted a perfectly good day."

"I know the feelin'. Spent yesterday and today shoppin', and the only thing I've accomplished is a headache from hell. But don't let Zane know that. Fucker's been done with his shoppin' since October."

Oh, yes. Travis had heard. Numerous times.

They inched along in the line as one person after another rattled off their extra shot, no foam, extra foam, add some vanilla cappu-latte whatevers.

"Find anything for the secret Santa?" Sawyer inquired.

Travis nodded. "Found that a month ago."

"Yeah, me, too." His brother's mischievous grin told Travis far more than he wanted to know. Sawyer was a legend when it came to his secret Santa gifts, and it was a damn near guarantee he'd make the recipient blush to the roots of their hair. That was saying something considering Travis owned a fetish resort and most of his brothers were into the lifestyle.

They took a minute to place their orders with the barista before joining the horde waiting for their cup of fancy joe.

"You know who I'm havin' the hardest time with?" Sawyer prompted. "Mom and Pop."

"Yeah, me, too." They were among the list of people he had to buy for, and Travis couldn't think of a single thing his parents wanted. Or needed, for that matter.

"We should've just taken a vacation. Hold up. I'll get it," Sawyer said before squeezing through the other patrons to grab Travis's black coffee when they called his name.

A vacation?

Why the hell hadn't he thought of that?

Sawyer returned to his side, eyebrows lowered as he passed over the cup. "What's on your mind?"

"A vacation," Travis said, meeting Sawyer's steel-blue eyes. "It's a fucking brilliant idea."

Sawyer's grin was slow and wide. "Yeah? And how to do you propose we pull that shit off? We've got what? Two weeks till Christmas. Ain't a room to be had at any resort worth a shit."

Travis pulled the lid off his coffee, blew on the steaming liquid as the idea took root in his head.

"Not to mention," Sawyer continued, "we've got an army we'd have to cart off. Airfare or, hell, even gas'll cost a fortune."

He turned to face Sawyer. "I know a resort with plenty of rooms."

Sawyer shook his head. "The B and B won't have the space to house us all."

"Not Rex's place." Definitely not enough space.

Sawyer's dark eyebrow quirked. "You're talkin' outta state? Like I said, ain't gonna—"

Travis smiled, perhaps for the first time in hours. "We won't have to leave Coyote Ridge."

Sawyer's eyebrows lowered, as though he was working to figure out the riddle. A second later, he barked a laugh, a sound much like a gunshot, causing several heads to turn. "AI? You wanna take Mom and Pop to the country's most profitable fetish resort?" Sawyer laughed again. "Man, I think that last clingy marble finally dropped right outta your head."

Travis took a sip of coffee, let the idea form in his head. Finally, he met Sawyer's amused gaze. "I'm serious. We'll shut it down for a week, make a few modifications, block off the fetish rooms. It could work."

His brother's expression sobered. "Actually ... that's not a bad idea."

"I know." Travis glanced at the counter, suddenly ready to get back to AI so he could put things in motion. "What the fuck kind of frou-frou drink did you order?"

"If I'm gonna pay eight bucks for a cup of coffee, I'm gonna get my money's worth."

"*I* paid for coffee," Travis told him.

Sawyer grinned. "Then I'll get *your* money's worth."

Thank the good Lord, they finally called Sawyer's name. When he sauntered over to get his dessert in the form of java, Travis moved to an empty table, set his cup down, and snatched his phone out of his pocket. He pulled up the group text he maintained with his brothers and Gage, then shot off an SOS, letting them know he required their presence at Moonshiners. Tonight. Seven o'clock.

Sawyer returned, staring at his phone. "You're bringin' them in on it, huh?"

Hell yeah he was.

And this would be the best damn Christmas they'd ever had.

Later that evening, Travis sat at a table in their favorite watering hole, his brothers scattered around the two four-tops they'd brought together, Gage at his side. He'd just laid out his plan and, as he'd expected, was met with a variety of expressions.

Kaleb, the easygoing one, looked as though he was on board for anything. Ethan, the normally dark, brooding one, gave an encouraging *why the hell not* shrug. Brendon appeared to be calculating the details in his head, likely trying to figure out whether his country music superstar wife would be in town that week. Braydon was glancing at Brendon, probably waiting for his twin to come to a conclusion. Sawyer, who was clearly on board, was watching the lot of them, waiting for someone to speak up. And Zane ... well, the youngest of them all was unhinging his jaw, gearing up for...

"You wanna do *what*?" Zane's blue-gray eyes bounced from face to face, clearly shocked no one else had spoken up.

"We'll shut it down for a week. Well, five days to be exact," Travis explained.

"And the clubs?" Zane inquired, referring to Covet and Crave, the two hot spots within the resort whose doors were open to the public.

"Won't be gettin' much action anyway," he told him. "And we'll have 'em back open in plenty of time for New Year's."

Zane's gaze shot to Ethan. "What about Walker Demo?"

Ethan shrugged at the same time Travis said, "Reese can clear the schedule."

"I think it's a brilliant idea," Kaleb said. "Keeps us all in one place and Travis is right. There's plenty of room."

"Who exactly are you invitin' to this thing?" Braydon asked.

"Family. Whoever's in Coyote Ridge, whoever wants to join us," Travis answered, then turned to Gage. "We'll wanna extend invitations to Jared and the Lambert crew."

Gage nodded. "Agreed."

"Also, the Caines," Travis added.

"Yep. We're gonna need a lot of help to get this underway," Gage said, his voice calm and cool, as though he expected Travis to come up with these off-the-wall ideas. Then again, he probably did. Travis had been known to throw a few curveballs over the years.

Travis met each stare, waited for official responses.

"I'm in," Kaleb said.

Zane peered around Braydon to look at Kaleb. "Of course you are."

Ethan was next with, "Count us in."

"Seriously?" Zane said, locking eyes with Ethan. "When's the last time you stepped foot in AI?"

"The grand opening," Travis supplied.

"Exactly," Zane stated. "Almost five years ago."

"So?" Ethan countered. "If you're takin' Mom and Pop, I figure I don't have to worry about seein' shit I have no business seein'."

Braydon and Brendon nodded at the same time, then in unison said, "Let's do this."

"I'm definitely game," Sawyer added.

Zane seemed to consider it. "Keep in mind, my lady just gave birth."

Yep. V had popped out her and Zane's fourth and final baby—another boy—just three days ago. Mom and baby were doing great.

"True," Kaleb said, looking at Gage. "We'll have to ensure she's set up in a suite."

"We can do that," Gage noted, his phone in his hand.

"Are you takin' notes?" Zane teased, bringing his beer bottle to his lips.

Gage smirked, then cut his eyes to Travis, a silent response of: *what do you think?*

Yep, Travis had to admit, he had the best husband in the history of husbands. The man knew him better than he knew himself. In fact, he wouldn't be surprised if Gage hadn't already planned for this. Maybe not a Christmas gathering, but he'd probably figured Travis would hijack the resort at some point.

"All right then," Travis told the group, setting down his beer and leaning forward. "We've got a shit ton to plan and not much time to do it."

GAGE MATTHEWS-WALKER HAD SUSPECTED HIS HUSBAND WAS up to something. The man had been off these past few days. Antsy. More so than normal, in any case. So he wasn't all that surprised when Travis threw out the idea of gathering the Walker crew at Alluring Indulgence Resort for a Christmas getaway.

Truth be told, it was a rather decent idea. The Walkers were known for their family gatherings. Hell, they still descended on Curtis and Lorrie's every Sunday for dinner, a tradition Lorrie had implemented many moons ago.

However, Gage also knew Travis wasn't going to settle for having a Christmas tree brought in and set up in the main floor recreation area. Oh, no. His overachieving husband was going to go all out, spare no expense in an effort to ensure his family had a grand ol' time.

"And a snow machine," Travis added, his fingers tapping on the steering wheel as he drove toward home.

"A snow machine?" Gage asked even as he added it in his notes app.

"Why not? The kids'll go apeshit for it."

True. Considering they didn't see much snow in their patch of Texas, a snow machine would be quite the treat.

"We'll set it up in the courtyard. Clear everything else out."

Gage tapped out the details, knowing he'd be the one delegating to those who'd signed up to help out.

"Make sure Kaden and Keegan know," Travis said, turning the wheel, directing the truck into the long driveway that led to their house. "Plus Rex and Rafe. Not sure they'll make it, but we can extend the invitation in any case."

The four names were added to the growing list.

"You gonna let Kylie in on this?" Gage asked, wanting to ensure they were on the same page before he did something stupid like let the cat out of the bag. Travis had already told his brothers to keep the details on the DL. No one was to know, but when it came to their wife, sometimes those rules didn't apply.

"Nope. Let it be a surprise."

Great. Gage knew how much Kylie loved surprises. About as much as a rabid case of chicken pox.

But this was Travis's plan, so Gage would follow it to the letter. Plus, he liked the idea of surprising Kylie. She worked so damn hard, maintaining her business restoring old houses while managing their household and raising five babies. She deserved to sit this one out and reap the benefits.

Travis stopped his truck behind Gage's, threw it in Park before launching himself out.

Gage smiled. The man was on a mission and everyone knew to stay out of Travis's way when he was in planning mode. For the next few days, there'd be no rest for the wicked. He'd long ago learned his husband's throttle was opened wide whenever he wanted something, and this would be no exception.

By the time Gage reached the front porch, Travis was already inside, walking through and flipping off all the lights as he went. Considering the time, Gage figured Kylie was passed out, perhaps on the sofa, where she generally napped on the nights they ended up coming home later than usual.

Gage dropped his keys and wallet on the table near the door, then flipped the deadbolt and set the security system. Though they didn't have much crime in their small backwoods town, Kylie insisted on the extra measure but only because it would alert them if a door or window was opened. It wasn't that she worried someone would come in, more so that a munchkin might get adventurous and attempt to slip outside to play in the backyard. After all, Kate had done it a couple of times when she was smaller.

Gage was staring down at his phone when he stepped into the living room, but that was as far as he made it before he was slammed up against the wall, the breath driven out of his lungs more from surprise than impact. His phone was plucked from his fingers and tossed to a chair.

"What are you doin'?" he asked Travis, keeping his voice low.

The man's eyes were hot as coals as they scanned his face briefly.

"Takin' what's mine," his husband whispered, then crushed his mouth to Gage's.

Christ Almighty, the man could kiss. Gage still remembered the first time Travis had kissed him. Very similar to this, in fact. Travis had surprised him then and many times in the past six years since they'd succumbed to their desires.

"Where's Kylie?" Gage asked, tilting his head to the side as Travis's teeth scraped sensually across his flesh.

"Sleepin'."

Which was the very reason Travis was molesting him in the living room. Had she been awake, Gage would've likely found the two of them on their bed, making out and waiting for him to join them. And while he loved those moments when the three of them came together, Gage couldn't deny he enjoyed the one-on-one time he got with each of them. He had the best of both worlds with Kylie and Travis. His wife was a sensual lover while his husband was the take-charge kind.

And right now, Travis was in take mode.

When Travis's mouth returned to his, Gage tugged at his T-shirt, desperate to get his hands on him. While he didn't mind Travis taking charge, Gage damn sure wasn't going to sit back and wait.

"Hold that thought," Travis rasped as he pulled away.

Or maybe he was.

Travis nodded. "This way."

Gage realized why Travis had jerked the reins: relocation.

They'd long ago learned that intimate moments required a bit of privacy. Hence the reason they'd closed off the formal living room, turning it into the adult playroom. Granted, it still looked like a living room with the couch and television, and sure, every now and again, the kiddos would chill in there and watch cartoons. But these days, the parents tended to sneak in there, close and lock the doors, and enjoy the pleasures they found in one another without the risk of a little one stumbling upon them.

When Gage stepped into the room, Travis closed the doors and flipped the lock before turning those intense blue-gray eyes on him once more. Gage backed up when Travis stalked him. His calves hit the edge of the sofa and he ass-planted in a hurry, bracing for the weight of his husband as Travis followed him down.

They shifted and moved until they were both laid out, chest to chest, mouth to mouth.

"I've been thinkin' about this all day," Travis whispered, pushing up to his knees and ripping off his T-shirt.

Gage struggled to do the same in his horizontal position. He'd barely managed to get his shirt over his head when Travis launched up off the couch, stripping off his boots and jeans in a mad rush. Before Gage could get his jeans unbuttoned, Travis was over him, one knee on the cushion beside Gage's head, one foot on the floor as he guided his thick cock into Gage's mouth.

"Ah, fuck yes," Travis hissed.

As he sucked Travis deep, Gage watched his husband's eyes roll back in his head, his pleasure evident, spurring Gage to work him over good.

Gage loved this side of Travis. The out-of-control side. It made its appearance less frequently these days, had been decreasing over the years, so he treasured the moments when Travis would let loose. There was no denying marriage and babies had changed all three of them, settled them as their family expanded, but underneath it all, Travis was still the same hungry beast he'd always been, and when Travis Walker wanted something, Kylie and Gage had learned to give in. After all, they reaped the benefits as well.

Travis groaned, his hips shifting forward and back as his cock tunneled in and out of Gage's mouth. He sucked and licked, slowly chipping away at Travis's restraint. It was a beautiful thing.

Of course, Travis wasn't a selfish lover, proving it when he pulled out of Gage's mouth and roughly stripped off the remainder of Gage's clothes. And when Travis's blazing-hot lips wrapped around his cock, his hips shot upward, head fell back as undiluted ecstasy blazed through his bloodstream.

It took effort, but Gage managed to hang on, distracting himself at one point by reaching for the drawer on the coffee table. He retrieved the tube of lubricant, leaving the drawer haphazardly open as the pleasure threatened to overwhelm him.

Travis didn't need directions, either. He released Gage's cock from between his lips, then moved over him, relieving Gage of the lubricant before their mouths crushed together once again.

Gage ran his hands over the taut muscles of Travis's back, pulling the man on top of him, relishing the weight, the warmth of the man he loved. He was vaguely aware of Travis shifting, his hand sliding between them, knew he was prepping his cock for entry.

Travis finally broke the seal on their mouths, pushing up to his knees. Gage didn't wait for instructions, pulling his knees toward his chest and making himself vulnerable to the man he loved. A minute later, Travis was pushing in deep, filling Gage's ass so perfectly. Their eyes met and held as Travis leaned over him, one hand braced on the back of the sofa, the other beside Gage's head.

"Fuck, you feel good," Travis said on a rough whisper.

Gage palmed his cock, stroking in the rhythm of Travis's long, deep thrusts. In their younger days, they could've done this for hours. Now they were both working toward the same goal: release before interruption. It was inevitable that someone would need something during their few stolen moments. Either work or kiddos, something generally needed their attention, so efficiency had become necessary.

And that was exactly what they did now only without the frantic edge. Travis moved inside him, deep and slow, their eyes locked, a wealth of emotion silently spoken between them as their bodies sought the pleasure of the other.

"I love you," Travis whispered.

Gage smiled. "Prove it."

Travis's eyes heated and then he gave Gage what he'd asked for, impaling him again and again, deeper, harder, faster. Gage was moaning softly, climbing that steep mountain until he was hanging on to the ragged edge by his fingernails.

"Come for me," Travis urged, his voice a low growl.

Gage didn't have to be told twice. He came, his cock jerking in his fist as Travis drove into him one final time and let himself go.

Chapter Two

"JUST OUT OF CURIOSITY, HOW DO YOU propose we explain to Zoey and V why the spa has no bookings for the week of Christmas?" Sawyer asked.

Travis sat behind his desk and stared at his brother. Sawyer was casually reclining on the black leather sofa, ankle crossed over his knee, his black Stetson dangling from his boot, one arm spanning the back of the sofa. Casual as you please, though his eyes said he was a bit nervous about the outcome of their new quest.

Since that was a damn good question, Travis could understand his reservations.

"We could just tell 'em we're cuttin' it to a skeleton crew for that week," Kaleb suggested. "I doubt my wife'll complain that she gets to stay home with the kids."

Sawyer laughed. "When are you gonna realize your wife goes to work to get away from those heathens?"

Being that Kaleb and Zoey had four kids, all barely a year apart, the oldest five, youngest two, there was no doubt Zoey sought an escape from time to time.

Kaleb grinned. "Yeah. You're probably right."

"Probably nothin'," Sawyer countered. "I asked Kennedy why she was so happy about those CrossFit classes she goes to and she told me exactly that. She went so far as to tell me it relaxes her. And we've only got two."

Kylie had mentioned the same thing to Travis. Ever since the woman had joined up with that cross-training shit, he had noticed she was smiling more. Stress relief, she called it. Travis had his own form of stress relief, and his husband and wife both participated as often as he could convince them.

His thoughts drifted to last night, having Gage beneath him...

"Travis?"

Jerking his attention from the gutter it was quickly shifting to, Travis looked at Kaleb. "Hmm?"

"Any suggestions?"

He peered down at the blotter on his desk, scanned the information jotted across every single day leading up to Christmas. "We're only shutting it down the two days before, the day of, and the two days after Christmas," he mused, looking up at Kaleb then Sawyer. "We'll just tell 'em we're letting the employees celebrate with their families this year. Paid time off. No one'll ask questions about that."

Sawyer nodded his head, his lips pursed. "Could work, sure."

The door to his office opened and Gage appeared, quickly scanning the other occupants before joining them.

"I need someone to get a combined list of everyone who's invited to this shindig," Gage said as he came over and perched on the corner of Travis's desk. "I figure you'll want me to reach out."

"Express how important this is to keep from the wives and kids," Travis told them. "I'd like them to be surprised if at all possible. I find out anyone leaks the information..."

Both Kaleb and Sawyer laughed.

"Oh, we know. Heads'll roll." Sawyer got to his feet. "I'd like you to include Jeff."

Gage once again had his phone in his hands, likely adding Sawyer's father-in-law to the list.

"Add Carl," Kaleb said. "The old fart'll get a kick out of it."

"Got it," Gage noted.

"Add Mack," Travis told him. "But under no circumstance is that shithead kid of his invited."

Travis normally didn't target people, but Daniel Schwartz was quickly becoming a major pain in the ass. At every turn, Mack's only child was attempting to direct Mack's life, using his father's love for him as a weapon. After Daniel had learned of Mack's sexual orientation—his own mother had kept Mack's secret for years, outing him when the boy turned eighteen—their relationship had been volatile, to say the least. After several years of keeping his distance from his father, looked as though Daniel was back, and of course, Mack was doing his best to get in the kid's good graces. Unfortunately, that required him to upend his entire life and pretend to be someone he wasn't. Travis didn't approve, but he knew it was none of his damn business. Didn't mean he had to be nice to the kid.

"I've also got Jared," Gage told them. "If his sisters-in-law and their old man want to come, I assume that's cool."

Travis nodded.

"I asked Ethan to talk to Kaden and Keegan," Gage continued.

"Invite Bristol," Travis suggested. The daycare owner had become a part of the Walker family, and since she had no family, he hoped she'd join them.

"I thought you promised not to meddle in relationships anymore," Kaleb teased.

"I'm not." Not entirely, anyway.

"I heard a rumor that Gerald and Sue Ellen were comin' down for Christmas. Probably need to reach out, get a head count if that's the case," Sawyer told Gage.

"Will do."

Travis looked at Gage. "You got the Caines, Right?"

He gave a curt nod. "I do."

Sawyer snapped his fingers. "Oh, and invite Greyson and Olivia."

Considering Greyson was Sawyer's best friend, Travis understood the request, so he nodded at Gage.

"What about Tavoularis?" Sawyer inquired, his eyes coming to rest on Travis.

"He's goin' to Dallas," Travis told him, referring to Reese, the man who was running the show at Walker Demolition. "He's already asked for the week off."

"You've got Jaxson and CJ on there, yeah?" Kaleb asked.

More cousins, more invites.

"Do now," Gage replied.

"I want you to figure out the food," Travis told Kaleb.

"You know Mom's gonna want to cook Christmas dinner."

Yep, Travis expected as much. "But that's the only time I want them to have to be in the kitchen. The plan's to get them to relax, not work."

Granted, that was easier said than done in the Walker clan.

"I'll make sure the chefs are aware of what we need," Kaleb confirmed. "You sure you don't want one of them on staff for that week?"

Travis shook his head. "They deserve time off, too."

"You can be in charge of decorations," Travis told Sawyer. "Get Braydon and Brendon on board. We'll all pitch in to decorate."

"And when do you plan to do that?"

"After all the guests check out on Sunday morning. And I want Zane to handle the accommodations. Have him wrangle Oscar in if he needs to," Travis said, referring to the hotel's concierge. "I want the rooms decorated, too. Trees in every occupied room."

"Every room." Kaleb whistled. "Travis's motto: go big or go home."

Travis wanted the kids to be surrounded by the sights and sounds of Christmas.

"You want me to see if Beau can help out?" Sawyer asked.

Travis shook his head. "That man spends his days caring for triplets. We'll let it be a surprise for him, too. He deserves it."

"Do I have a budget for decorations?" Sawyer asked.

Travis leaned back in his chair. "Spare no expense, but don't be stupid about it."

His brother grinned. "Unlimited funds. Yeah, I'd say this is gonna be a kick-ass vacation."

That was Travis's plan and he knew with his brothers' help, they'd make it happen.

As Zane drove from the resort back to his house, he found himself smiling. Then again, that was a frequent occurrence for him. Getting home to his wife and boys had been the highlight of every day. Not that he didn't enjoy his job. How could he not? But it didn't hold a candle to how good it felt to be home with them.

He parked his truck behind V's Ford Expedition, snatched his phone from the center console, and hopped out. He launched himself over the two steps leading to the porch, then paused a second to calm himself. Never knew what he'd find on the other side of that door, and the last thing he wanted to do was cause chaos.

With a deep breath, he reached for the knob, turned it, then stepped into the darkened interior.

He set his coat on the hat rack, pulled his jacket off and hung it on the hook on the wall, then deposited his keys in the clear crystal bowl on the shelf up high. They'd had to resort to that earlier this year, back when Asher turned two. The kid had found it fascinating to steal the car keys and make the horns honk using the key fob.

"Hey, baby," Zane greeted V when he joined her in the living room.

His beautiful wife was sitting on the sofa, Dustin swaddled in a blue blanket, tucked securely in her arms. Zane smiled as he stared down at the sweet boy.

"How'd he do today?" he asked, keeping his voice low so as not to disturb him.

"Perfect. Where're the other rug rats?"

Zane shifted his attention to her. "Kaleb invited Reid to spend the night. Sawyer has Asher, and Brendon's keeping Theo."

"That's awfully generous of them."

Not to mention necessary. Being that V and Dustin had only been home for two days, Zane had hoped she'd get as much sleep as possible. He didn't mind getting up with Dustin during the night, but it became something else entirely when the baby woke up the other boys, as they'd learned with Theo. A midnight feeding could turn into a playdate, and Zane was hoping for a couple of days without it.

Granted, he would miss those rug rats like crazy.

Funny, before V, Zane had never figured he was the settling-down type, but the woman had knocked him for a loop, and he'd fallen fast. Now, six years later, he had four healthy boys and the most beautiful wife on the planet. Couldn't ask for more than that.

"You wanna hold him?"

Zane grinned wide. Of course he did.

Moving around the sofa, he eased down beside V and took the tiny bundle from her arms, cradling Dustin against his chest. He tossed his other arm over V's shoulders and pulled her into him. He stared at the television, though he wasn't seeing what was on the screen. No, his mind was on the Christmas vacation Travis had come up with and all the boxes that had to be checked before it could happen.

While he'd been skeptical, Zane had to admit, the idea was brilliant. Plus, he knew his oldest brother. Travis would put together a shindig to rival all. He could already picture Reid, Asher, and Theo running amok, the grandparents nearby, cousins all around them. He figured by the time it was over, they'd likely need a real vacation, but he didn't mind.

Now the question was, could they pull it off?

"What are you thinkin' about?" V asked, her voice raspy, as though she was drifting in and out of sleep.

"Christmas," he admitted, keeping to the truth as much as he could.

"It's not far off, huh?"

"It'll be here before you know it." He pressed his lips to V's forehead. "When's the last time he ate?"

"He'll be waking up any minute now."

"Why don't you go take a nap in the bedroom. At least until dinner. I'll feed him, then get you up in a couple of hours. How's Salisbury steak and mashed potatoes sound?"

V snuggled closer. "I won't say no to either. The nap or the food."

As V got to her feet and headed out of the living room, Zane's eyes caressed every inch of her. Still the most beautiful woman on the planet.

Chapter Three

Sunday, December 22, 2019

WHILE GAGE WASN'T ONE TO DOUBT TRAVIS or his various schemes, he had to admit, he'd had some concerns on whether or not they'd be able to pull off a Christmas vacation that would live up to Travis's expectations.

Now as he stood overlooking the main recreation area, he was glad to say his concern had been unnecessary. Should've known the Walker brothers would give two hundred percent to this endeavor. They always did. Without a hitch, at that.

Well, that wasn't exactly true. There'd been a couple of glitches they'd dealt with, but luckily they'd hit the ground running from the minute Travis decided to go forward with his modified version of Sawyer's idea. After they'd smoothed out the rough edges, everything had come together perfectly. The decorations were pretty damn close to perfect throughout the resort, including the restaurant they would be taking over for their formal meals. All twenty of the rooms that would be occupied had been given a holiday face-lift and hopefully would meet the standards of the twenty-five kiddos who'd be participating in the festivities.

Come tomorrow morning, this place would be filled, and Gage couldn't wait to see his kids' faces. And Kylie's.

How they'd managed to keep the details from the wives and husband—in Ethan's case—Gage would never know. The only positive was that they'd only had eleven days to plan and get the gears moving. Any longer and he doubted they'd have kept it under wraps.

Gage's cell phone rang, so he tugged it out of his pocket.

"Hey, baby," he greeted Kylie.

"Just wonderin' when y'all'll be home. Figured I'd make shepherd's pie for dinner."

"Sounds perfect." Not to mention, it was one of the few meals that all the kids ate. Most nights they were preparing at least three different entrees, catering to the kids' varied tastes. "We should be outta here in half an hour."

"Perfect. I'll see you then. Love you."

"Love you, too."

After tucking his phone away, Gage headed to Travis's office, worried that his husband had buried himself in work when they'd agreed to go home and surprise Kylie and the kids with their official invitations to the holiday escape.

"You about ready?" he asked when he stepped inside.

"Yep. Two seconds."

Gage knew that Travis's time was in football minutes, so he perched on the arm of the oversized leather chair and waited while the man finished typing.

"You know Kylie's waitin' for us," Gage told him after a good five minutes had passed.

"Yep. Two seconds."

Gage smiled. "She's naked."

Travis's eyes shot up. "No she's not."

Chuckling, Gage got to his feet. "You'll never know unless we go home and find out."

With a huff, Travis tapped a few more keys, then closed the lid on his laptop. He tucked it into the leather bag he used to carry it to and from the office, then got to his feet.

"She's gonna be naked before the night's over," Travis mumbled as they headed out the door.

Gage sure as hell hoped that was the case.

Four hours later, Gage was stepping out of Kade's room, easing the door closed behind him.

It had taken a good half hour to get the three-year-old to stop talking about what he was going to do on their vacation, but finally, he'd talked himself out. Travis had tackled getting the girls settled for the night, which likely took as much effort, if not more, than getting Kade down. Kylie had tucked Haden in when the boy had nearly fallen asleep in his mashed potatoes and peas two hours ago. And seven-month-old Maddox had conked out roughly an hour ago, which was a surprise considering he was their night owl.

Now, if the five of them would sleep through the night, they'd have it made.

As he passed all the bedrooms on the way to his, he noticed all the doors were closed, which was a good sign the kiddos were finally asleep.

But someone was up based on the sounds coming from the master bedroom.

The door was open a crack, so Gage paused to peek inside. Sure enough, Kylie was on the bed, Travis's much bigger body covering her as he worked to strip her. Not wanting to be left out, he slipped inside, closing and locking the door behind him. Last thing they needed was Kate walking in on them, which had happened before. Not the most comfortable feeling in the world to realize your five-year-old was getting an eyeful of something she didn't need to know about until she was thirty or so.

Gage didn't interrupt the make-out session, choosing instead to move around to his side of the bed, never looking away from Travis and Kylie. Although he enjoyed the hell out of being the filling in their sexy sandwich, he could admit he had a bit of a voyeuristic streak. Moments like these, when he could observe, were a rare treat.

Of course, he didn't go unnoticed. The moment Travis inched down Kylie's body, her cornflower-blue eyes settled on him. She smiled as Travis worked her leggings down her hips before tugging them off and tossing them across the room. Their husband settled between her spread thighs, used his fingers to part the glistening folds of her sex before he leaned down and licked her.

Gage's cock kicked behind his fly, the damn thing going rock hard at the sight of them together.

"You've got on too many clothes," Kylie said on a moan.

As he worked to remedy that, he continued to watch Travis feasting on her pussy, his tongue working her into a frenzy. Before he could send her over the edge, Gage intervened.

"My turn," he said as he lay on the bed beside Kylie. "Come sit on my face."

She didn't hesitate, getting to her knees before she straddled his chest. He loved the rich scent of her arousal. Even more than that, though, he loved the taste of her on his tongue. Giving her full control, Gage teased her clit as she fucked his face. The only time he paused was when Travis took his cock into his blazing hot mouth. He moaned, then slid his arms around Kylie's thighs, pulling her onto his mouth. It took effort to concentrate, but somehow he managed.

When Kylie cried out, he released his grip on her thighs, allowing her to shift down his body.

"I want both of you tonight," she said, her voice loud enough for Travis to hear.

A rough growl came from behind her at the same time Gage groaned. He fucking loved being buried to the hilt inside her at the same time Travis was.

"Put me inside you," he commanded.

She didn't hesitate, inching down on his cock, her silky heat enveloping him.

With his eyes on her, Gage watched as Kylie rode him. She didn't rush, giving Travis time to prepare himself to take her tight little ass.

Gage felt the mattress shift seconds before Kylie was leaning forward, her beautiful tits crushed to his chest. He took her mouth then, his tongue delving inside as he rocked his hips. She moaned softly into his mouth when Travis's cock pushed inside her ass. Gage could feel the hard ridge of his erection as he slowly inched in deeper.

As they'd done many times over the years, they found their rhythm, the two of them alternating as they fucked their beautiful wife, crushing her between them. She moaned and sighed, whimpered and begged, driving them higher and higher until they were in a race to the finish line. Gage held back as long as he could, wanting both of them to come before he did. Kylie detonated first, her pussy milking his cock. A ragged groan escaped him, followed quickly by Travis's deep grunt of release.

Only then did Gage give in.

TRAVIS WOKE TO THE SOUND OF MADDOX'S faint whimper coming through the baby monitor on his nightstand. He hurried to turn it off so that it didn't wake Kylie or Gage as he slipped out of bed.

Groggy from sleep, he stumbled a few steps on his way to the baby's room. By the time he got to the door, he was wide-awake and smiling. Most people wouldn't understand the excitement he felt when he had a few minutes to spend with his sons and daughters alone. These days the one-on-one time was limited. Usually, when Maddox woke up, Haden wasn't far behind. And in half an hour or so, the rest of the kids would be bouncing around the house, eager for the day to get underway.

"Hey, little man," Travis greeted his son when he peered down into the crib to see Maddox staring up at him.

When the baby smiled, his heart turned over in his chest.

"You hungry?" he asked as he reached for a diaper and went through the motions of getting Maddox's butt into something more comfortable.

By the time he was finished, his seven-month-old was grinning wide, giggling every so often as Travis kept up the running monologue.

"All right. You're good to go."

Travis lifted the little guy into his arms, then carried him down the stairs and into the kitchen.

"Scrambled eggs?" he asked the squirmy boy before settling him into his high chair. "You got it."

After peeling a banana and giving Maddox pieces of it, Travis moved on to preparing scrambled eggs. Breakfast for eight required finesse and Travis had long ago mastered the art. With Kylie's help, of course. She was a natural, while Travis still fumbled around on occasion. So maybe *mastered* wasn't the right word.

Of course, bacon was a requirement when scrambling eggs, so he started that process and grabbed some bread, slipped it into the toaster. It took roughly half an hour for him to get it all prepared, and by then, he'd already carted Haden down. He figured Kate, Avery, and Kade would be along shortly. His kids had a keen sense of smell and they always knew when breakfast was ready.

"Hey, shorty," Travis greeted Kate, the last of the five to make her way down to the kitchen. "Do me a favor?"

"What, Daddy-O?"

"Go wake up Mom and Dad."

"I wanna wake 'em up!" Kade squealed.

"All right. Go on."

While Kate and Kade shot up the stairs like a stampede of buffalo, Travis got Avery settled with a glass of orange juice.

"Are we gonna go to vacation today?" she asked, beaming up at him.

"We are. Just as soon as we pack our stuff." Before Avery could launch out of her chair, he settled her with a gentle hand on her shoulder. "Not yet, baby girl. Let's eat breakfast first."

"I'm not hungry," she countered as she snagged a slice of bacon off the plate in the center of the table.

"Then humor me," he told her. "Daddy-O wants you to eat one piece of bacon and three bites of eggs. Can you do that?"

Her mouth was already full when she added, "Mm-hmm."

Kate and Kade returned a minute later, Gage following close behind.

"Mornin'," Travis greeted, making his way over and kissing Gage on the mouth. Of course, he lingered a bit too long and earned a snicker or two from Kade and Avery.

"You two need to get a room," Kate said.

Travis chuckled as he pulled away. "I really think we should limit her time with Zane."

Gage laughed, pouring three mugs of coffee when the pot gurgled its completion.

Three hours later, after baths and showers were taken, suitcases were packed and repacked, and they'd returned to the house only once to grab Avery's security blanket, they were making the five-minute trek to the resort. By the time they'd pulled up to the front doors, the kids were making more racket than a daycare full of toddlers.

Gage hurried off to grab a luggage cart, returning so they could pile everything on while Kylie led the kids inside. Travis noticed Kennedy's Lexus and Zoey's SUV already parked in the lot, so he figured they'd be entertained for a while.

Since everything had been prepped last night, they simply had to retrieve the key cards to their room from the concierge desk, then make their way up the elevator to their floor.

"Adjoining rooms," Travis mused as Gage led the way inside. "Smart thinking."

"Doesn't mean we won't have a bed full of kids, but I figured maybe Maddox would get some sleep this way."

Yeah, Travis wasn't sure sleep was on the agenda. Then again, after a full day of excitement, he figured they might surprise him.

Rather than head back down, Travis worked alongside Gage to get their clothes unpacked, toiletries moved to the bathroom, portable cribs set up for Haden and Maddox. While they'd brought an extra one for Avery—just in case—Travis tucked it into the closet. Their youngest daughter was very independent, and he figured she'd balk at the idea of not sleeping in the big bed with Kade and Kate. He figured they'd learn through trial and error whether it needed to be dragged back out.

"All right," Gage said, hands on his hips as he surveyed the room. "I think we're ready to kick this thing off."

"Yeah?" Travis moved toward him. "I was thinkin' perhaps we could steal a few minutes."

Gage's eyes glittered with heat. "What did you have in mind?"

Travis proceeded to show him the best way to steal those minutes.

Chapter Four

Monday, December 23, 2019

"THIS IS INCREDIBLE," KENNEDY SAID, HER VOICE full of wonder and awe.

Sawyer couldn't hide how pleased he was to hear her say that. The past couple of weeks had been chaotic, to say the least, and now that the day had finally arrived, he wasn't sure it was going to settle much. But it helped to get her approval.

"You came up with this idea?" she said, turning to face him.

He peered down into her smiling face. "Oh, no. Not *this*," he admitted. "I simply planted the seed about a vacation. This sprouted in Travis's head all on its own."

Kennedy glanced back to where Matthew was hovering over Brody as the boys interacted with the other kids. Big brother was always on the lookout for little brother. Kind of reminded Sawyer of Travis.

"Well, nonetheless, it's rather impressive. He went all out, huh?"

"That he did." Hell, if it hadn't been for the rest of them reining Travis in a bit, they would've likely had Santa and his elves taking up residence for the duration. Luckily for them all, Santa would only be joining them for a short time tomorrow.

Catching the sight of his father-in-law moving toward them, Sawyer put his arm over Kennedy's shoulder and tugged her into his side.

"This is right out of a fairy tale," Jeff Endsley said, nodding toward the area where all the kids were currently in the process of various creative endeavors. "How tall is that tree, anyway? As big as the Rockefeller tree?"

Sawyer laughed. "Not quite. But that's because Braydon and Brendon picked it out. Not Travis."

"Where is he, anyway?" Kennedy peered up at him. "I haven't seen him or Gage."

"They're around here somewhere." Probably snuck off to have a little quality time. Something Sawyer intended to do in the very near future.

As though reading his mind—although that would've been extremely creepy—Jeff turned to face them. "Figured I could spend a couple of hours with the boys. Then I've got to get back to work."

"Did you at least get settled in your room?" Sawyer inquired.

"I did. I'll be in and out, though. Still on duty for the week, but figured I'd hang out to see the munchkins."

"I know they'll be happy to know you're here," Kennedy told him. "Matthew's been tellin' Brody all about how Papa's comin' to play at the vacation."

Jeff grinned, more than a little pride on his face.

"Would you mind keeping an eye on them for a bit?" Sawyer asked, wanting to take advantage of the opportunity, of course.

Jeff's all-knowing eyes scanned his face. "Sure. But don't go far."

"Thanks. I just want to show Kennedy around."

Jeff shook his head as he walked away. "Sure you do."

"Show me around?" Kennedy chuckled. "You forget that I stop by this place once a week."

Oh, no. He would never forget how his amazing wife brought him lunch once a week here at the resort. In fact, he looked forward to Tuesdays for that very reason.

"So what are you plannin' to show me, Mr. Walker?"

"Remember how Travis wanted to lock up all the theme rooms?"

"Yes."

Sawyer dipped his hand in his pocket and pulled out a key. "I have this."

His sexy wife smiled as he'd hoped she would.

A few minutes later, Sawyer had snuck them into one of the private rooms on the second floor.

"An office?" Kennedy asked as she peered around.

"*Pretend* office. Won't find anything in the desk. Well, except condoms and lube."

"What about the printer?" She motioned toward the far corner.

"Fake."

Kennedy turned to face him as she took a seat on the top of the desk. "Do you have this office fantasy often?"

Sawyer didn't miss a beat, moving to stand between her legs, brushing her long auburn hair back over her shoulders. "Every now and then." He leaned down and kissed the soft skin of her neck. "Remember that time in your office? Back when you were trying to pretend you didn't like me?"

Kennedy chuckled as she tilted her head to give him better access. "Oh, I remember. That was a lifetime ago."

"Sometimes it seems that way." Sawyer trailed his lips over her jaw, her cheek, until he was hovering over her mouth. "I figured we could reenact that day."

"My memory's not that good," she said on a laugh.

"Then we'll make it up as we go along."

Sawyer licked her lower lip before sliding his tongue inside her mouth. Kennedy leaned into him, a move he'd gotten used to over the years. Though they didn't happen nearly as often as he would've liked. Kennedy was going full-steam at her veterinary clinic and Sawyer spent roughly fifty hours a week right here at the resort. When they finally made it home at the end of a long day, they were wrangling two little monsters and Buster. By the time they were ready for bed, one or both of them usually conked out before the lights dimmed all the way.

"I want you naked," he whispered when he pulled his mouth from hers.

"Do you now?"

He met her pretty gray eyes and smiled. "Shall I do the honors?"

"Yes, please."

As she reclined on the desk, Sawyer took his time, removing her clothes piece by piece as he sampled every inch of her with his lips.

"Lift," he instructed as he slipped his fingers into the elastic band of her panties.

When she did, he slowly slid the silk down her thighs, her calves, over her feet. As he let them drop to the floor, his eyes locked on that sweet spot between her legs. And when Kennedy teased him, spreading her knees wide, Sawyer groaned his approval.

"Christ Almighty, woman. You're gonna be the death of me."

Leaning down, he used his fingers to part her delicate folds before grazing her clit with his tongue.

"Oh, God," Kennedy moaned. "It's been far too long since you've done that."

Indeed it had.

Which was why he made up for all that lost time by feasting on her for long minutes. He would work her to the edge, then ease back only to do it again and again until Kennedy's hands fisted in his hair as she held him to her. Sawyer flicked her clit ruthlessly, giving her what she needed.

Before the last syllable of his name had fallen from her lips, Sawyer had freed his cock from his jeans, pulled her hips to the edge of the desk, and plunged into her warm, welcoming heat. With his hands on the backs of her thighs, he drove deep inside her again and again, the frantic need consuming him as it always did. Even all these years later, Sawyer couldn't get enough of Kennedy.

"Sawyer ... oh, God. I'm close."

Yeah, so was he, but he wasn't going to come yet.

He impaled her over and over, loving the way her pussy clamped down on him as she orgasmed. It wasn't until she was out of breath from the multiple times he sent her over that he chased his own release, shifting his hand so he could thumb her clit.

Kennedy cried out his name as she'd done back before they had kids, without worry someone would hear. It was the trigger that sent him soaring. His cock pulsed deep inside her as his hips stilled, his eyes caressing every soft, sweet inch of her.

"I sure hope we get to do that again," his wife said with a twinkle in her eyes.

"I'll make sure of it."

And that was a promise he fully intended to keep.

GOD ONLY KNEW WHY MICHAEL "MACK" SCHWARTZ had accepted this invitation.

Dropping his ass to the fancy king-sized bed, he stared around the large room. It was a nice hotel, he'd give the Walkers that. From what he could tell, they'd spared no expense for the thick down comforter, the fancy wall coverings, expensive art, even the six-foot-tall Christmas tree in the corner. Hell, the four-hundred-square-foot space beat the crap out of the two-bedroom house he'd lived in for the past thirty-some years.

He should've been sitting at home, staring at the television. The television he hadn't upgraded since the early 2000s. Wouldn't matter what was on the screen, it would've been the wise choice. But, no. For some fool reason, he'd been feeling melancholy as of late and had practically leapt at the chance to get out of the house, somewhere that wasn't Moonshiners. Which explained why his ass was here at this monstrous resort.

Okay, that wasn't entirely true.

There was another reason.

Though Mack loved his son, Daniel was starting to wreak havoc on his life, and Mack had wanted the chance to clear his head, to figure out the best course of action to take, because that was the one thing he was certain about. He had to make some changes. One way or another.

He'd initially thought it would be easy to do as Daniel asked, to modify his life so the boy would be back in it. That was the only thing he'd ever wanted anyway, to be a father, to watch his only child grow up.

So when had things gotten so difficult?

The question was rhetorical, really. Mack knew exactly when.

First, the boy had made him feel guilty about *who* he was, voicing his displeasure for the fact Mack was gay. Of course, Mack blamed his ex for letting that feral cat out of the bag. While she'd demanded a divorce when he'd revealed to her his sexual orientation—rightfully so—she'd promised to keep his secret from the boy in an effort not to cause conflict between them. He should've known the vindictive woman would eventually out him. That revelation had sent Daniel in the opposite direction and Mack had lost his relationship with his son years ago.

It wasn't until recently that the boy had come back into his life. Since then, Mack had been doing his best to make up for lost time.

He pushed to his feet, marched to the bathroom, and stared at the man in the mirror. His beard had long ago turned gray along with his hair, which could definitely use a trim. At least he had hair, he thought.

Not that it really mattered. Who the hell was he trying to impress?

In an effort to appease Daniel, Mack had gone so far as to call off the one and only relationship he'd ever had that made him happy because his son was a homophobe. That was bad enough. Now the kid wanted him to sell the bar, move to Austin, and spend the rest of his days doing God only knew what. They hadn't made it that far in the conversation, but Mack figured Daniel would tell him soon enough.

"Fucking Austin," he grumbled, hating the idea of living in a city packed with people.

But he wasn't here to think about that. No, instead of letting the kid run roughshod over him, Mack had accepted the Walker invitation to this Christmas business, leaving Moonshiners in Rafe Sharpe's willing and capable hands so he could get away from the pressure cooker his life had become. For the time being, of course. Just for the next couple of nights. He'd needed the break, and since Rafe hadn't balked when Mack asked him to fill in as bartender, he had no excuses. Probably helped that Bailey Weber was his faithful waitress and there was no doubt Rafe had a thing for the young woman.

He wondered what those kids would think if they learned Mack was holed up in the hotel room rather than in the fray as he'd promised he would be.

Giving his reflection one last look, he turned and headed for the door. Mack sighed as he stepped out into the hallway, glancing both directions before forcing his legs to carry him to the elevator. By the time he made it to the main floor, he felt as though someone had a plastic bag over his head and was holding it tight around his neck. No doubt Jeff was here, probably having a grand ol' time with his grandsons. Mack had no fucking business being here, and every step felt as though he was seconds from stepping off the plank into the deep, dark abyss.

Rather than march into the madness, Mack kept to the perimeter of the space filled to bursting with little ones. God, when was the last time he'd been around kids?

He couldn't help but smile as he watched the kiddos enjoying themselves. They were making their way through various stations. Some were coloring pictures of Santa, others getting their faces painted, and a couple were erecting an enormous block tower that was beginning to wobble at the base.

It brought back so many memories.

Truth was, he missed those days.

Back when Daniel had been a little boy, Mack had spent every possible minute with the kid. His ex-wife had hated him with a passion to rival all, but she'd held up her end of the bargain, allowing Mack to spend time with his son. In the fall, they'd sat beneath the bright stadium lights and watched the high school football team battle it out with their rivals. In the spring, they'd checked out the baseball team. And in between, they'd gone to every festival and carnival the small town had put on.

In a word, life had been good.

"Well, I'll be damned."

Mack swallowed hard, planted a wide smile on his face, and turned to face Travis Walker.

"I'm damn glad you made it, man," Travis said, holding out a hand in greeting.

Mack shook it. "Quite the party you put together."

Travis's smile lit up his entire face as he scanned the enormous room. "I think they're enjoying it."

There was no doubt about that.

As they looked on, one of the little girls who was getting her face painted decided to do some painting of her own. Her chubby hand found a puddle of blue paint, and she proceeded to put a smudged handprint on the face of the woman doing the painting. It earned her a laugh from the woman as well as from Mack.

He was still grinning when a man walked right in his line of sight.

Not just any man.

Jeff Endsley.

The one and only love of Mack's life.

Mack's breath caught in his throat when Jeff's eyes shifted to him, a surprised expression crossing his handsome face.

"I think that's my cue to go," Travis said, and Mack knew he wasn't waltzing over to help with the painting child.

Oh, no. Never that simple.

Jeff was coming over.

For a brief moment, Mack considered fleeing. Running far and fast so he didn't have to face the man he'd walked away from all those years ago. The same man he thought about in the dark of night when the cold loneliness consumed him.

"Mack."

His voice was gruff when he said, "Jeff."

Their eyes remained locked as they stood there. Considering his lungs weren't working appropriately, it felt like an eternity to Mack. Yet he couldn't seem to look away. It had been so damn long since he'd gotten a glimpse of the sexy sheriff. Ever since Mack had called off their relationship, Jeff had made a point not to come into Moonshiners unless he was called there for a disturbance.

"You look good," Mack whispered.

Evidently, Jeff hadn't expected him to say that, because Jeff's wary brown eyes widened ever so slightly.

"I ... uh ... I should go," Mack blurted, though he wasn't sure where he would go.

Jeff surprised him then, stepping in close and staring down into his eyes. "Don't leave on my account."

Mack's lungs constricted even as he inhaled Jeff's familiar scent. It was the cologne Mack had bought for him years ago, and the rich, sultry scent teased his nostrils, hardened his entire body.

"I'll see you later," Jeff whispered before sauntering toward the doors.

Turning so that he didn't lose sight of him, Mack finally realized what he wanted for Christmas this year.

The one thing he never should've let go of.

Chapter Five

"WELL, WOULD YOU LOOK AT THAT," KEEGAN whispered from beside Kaden.

Curious as to what his twin was looking at, Kaden Walker followed his brother's gaze and was damn glad he had.

There, looking as beautiful as ever, was Bristol Newton. Her hair was pulled back in a ponytail, her face beaming as she allowed Travis's oldest daughter, Kate, to lead the way to a table.

"I thought she said she wasn't comin'," Keegan noted, eyes tracking her as she moved.

She had, but Kaden was glad to see she'd changed her mind.

A little surprised, but not the least bit disappointed, Kaden smiled when Kate stopped at the side of Keegan's chair.

"Uncle Keegan, can we sit with you?"

Keegan grinned. "Of course you can, darlin'."

Kate peered up at Bristol. "Can we, Miss Bristol?"

Kaden was watching Bristol's face when she looked over at him, her light blue eyes a tad wary. "Sure."

Since Kaden and Keegan were sitting opposite one another at the square table, both girls ended up sitting at each side.

"I'm glad you could make it," Kaden said softly when Bristol eased into her chair.

The plate she'd gotten at the dinner buffet had small amounts of everything. Spaghetti and meatballs, ravioli, beef pasta, and a chicken strip. Looked as though the woman liked her carbs and Kaden was happy to see that. The last girl he and his brother had dated refused to eat carbs of any kind, insisting they went right to her hips. Truth was, Kaden preferred a curvy girl to those stick-thin types. And Bristol was curvy in all the right places, which was one of the many reasons she tripped his trigger.

"Daddy-O said we're gonna have a snow machine tomorrow," Kate informed them as she gnawed on a chicken strip.

"Yeah?" Keegan asked, leaning toward her as though her words were what he longed for.

Probably were, now that Kaden thought about it. Keegan was the reigning king of the kids. Granted, that was only because Beau had taken a step back since the triplets were born. Keegan hadn't missed a beat, inserting himself so that he was the fun "uncle" even if the kids didn't realize he was really a second cousin.

"I'm gonna be checkin' that out," Keegan told her. "You with me?"

"Oh, yeah." Kate grinned wide.

Keegan turned his attention to Bristol. "What about you? Wanna join us tomorrow?"

Bristol's cheeks turned a rosy pink. Kaden had noticed that was a regular occurrence with her, especially when one or both of them attempted to chat her up. Of course, she did her best to keep her distance, but it wasn't easy considering she'd become an honorary Walker over the past couple of years. Not only because she owned and ran the only daycare center in Coyote Ridge and interacted with nearly all of Curtis and Lorrie's twenty-three grandkids. She was more than merely a babysitter, which was why the Walkers had invited her here this weekend.

"Sure," Bristol said, her eyes remaining on Kate as though the little girl had extended the offer. "If you'll let me."

"Yes!" Kate squealed. "We're gonna have so much fun."

With that, the rug rat launched out of her chair and tore ass across the room, leaving the three of them sitting there. Kaden had to admit, it was a tad awkward. Everything he would've normally said to engage a woman, to lure her into their bed, wasn't appropriate for this setting. Not any setting with Bristol.

Not because Bristol wasn't exactly their type and not because he didn't fantasize about having her crushed between them.

Oh, no. That wasn't the problem at all.

Kaden had been thinking about Bristol for what felt like an eternity even though he'd yet to taste those sweet, lush lips. He'd imagined stripping her naked, taking her between them, and spending hours bringing her to climax again and again. Sometimes it was the only thing he could think about.

And not appropriate.

For one, Bristol Newton wasn't the one-and-done sort. She wasn't the type of woman a man took to bed and walked away from come daylight.

Truth was, Kaden was all right with that. And under the right circumstances, he was sure Keegan would be as well.

But, as usual, Bristol had that gleam of uncertainty in her eyes when she looked at them. As though they were dangerous beasts and she was seconds away from being devoured.

"So ... are you having a good time?" Bristol asked, her gaze on her food even as she spoke.

"We are," Kaden told her. "You?"

She nodded.

Keegan pushed his chair back. "I'm gonna grab dessert. Want anything?"

"I'm good," Kaden told him, knowing his brother was purposely stepping away to put Bristol at ease.

"Bristol?"

Her eyes slid up to Keegan, another polite smile forming. "Oh, no. I'm fine. Thank you."

Finally alone with her for the first time in months, Kaden was at a loss for words.

"I heard the adults are gonna get together to hang out later," Bristol said. "At the bar downstairs."

"Are you invitin' us to join you?" he asked, falling back on his flirtatious nature.

Those rosy patches returned to her cheeks. "No. That's... I was just making conversation."

"Because we'd love to," he said softly.

Her eyes flicked up to his face and he saw the interest there. Of course, it disappeared almost instantly, but that was normal, too. Kaden had gotten used to Bristol keeping him at arm's length.

"I..." Bristol laughed, her gaze dropping to her plate. "It wasn't an invite, I promise."

Maybe not, but Kaden wasn't above taking an opportunity when it presented itself.

He was a Walker, after all.

―――――――――――

TWO HOURS LATER, BRISTOL WAS JOINING THE handful of people who'd come down for a nightcap.

It was against every instinct, but she'd done it to prove a point. It hadn't escaped her that Kaden Walker had tossed out his line and was attempting to reel her in. And she'd come here tonight to prove she wasn't going to take the bait. As far as she was concerned, Kaden and Keegan were like family. Like brothers. She thought of them the same way she thought of the rest of the Walkers.

Keep telling yourself that.

Yeah, yeah, yeah. That wasn't anywhere near the truth, and she couldn't even lie to herself.

So what's the harm in seeing where it might lead? Hmm? One night between them. You know you want to.

She ignored that annoying inner voice as she stepped over to the bar. Bristol smiled when she realized Mack was behind it, pouring drinks as he normally did at Moonshiners.

"They roped you into bartending?" she asked, relaxing a bit.

He gave a rare smile. "I volunteered. I don't do well with idle time."

"I know the feelin'," she admitted. "Can I get a vodka cranberry?"

"Comin' right up." Mack grabbed a bottle off the top shelf. "Enjoyin' yourself so far?"

"I am." It was true, though she'd been skeptical when Kaleb had extended the offer.

Truth was, Bristol had figured they'd invited her to help out with the kids. Considering there were a couple dozen, she couldn't very well blame them. But that wasn't the case. She was interacting with the kids because she wanted to, not because she was obligated. Granted, all those little ones were tucked into their beds at this point, or getting close to it. Which explained why the bar was so empty. Someone had to stay up in the rooms with them, and it appeared the dads had been nominated.

"Here you are," Mack said, passing over her drink. He nodded behind her. "Looks like Zoey's tryin' to get your attention."

With her drink in hand, Bristol turned. Sure enough, Zoey lifted a hand and waved her over. As she moved to the table where Zoey, Kylie, Jessie, and Cheyenne were sitting, she couldn't help scanning the area for Kaden and Keegan. It was a natural reaction, she told herself. Self-preservation and all that.

"We're so glad you could make it after all," Jessie said when she took her seat. "Zoey told me you didn't think you'd be able to get off work."

Yeah, that was a conditioned response whenever she wanted to get out of doing something. And it wasn't that she didn't enjoy spending time with the Walkers. They'd been good to her, inviting her to their family functions as though she belonged there. However, deep down, she knew she didn't, and she hated the idea of being an extra wheel.

"My assistant manager agreed to handle things. At least for the next two days. I'll have to get back on Thursday."

"Well, at least you're here now," Kylie said, then lifted her drink. "Here's to relaxing."

The five of them toasted before easing back into their chairs.

"I still don't know how they managed to pull this off," Zoey said, peering around at the decor. "Without any of us figuring it out."

"Sneaky husbands, that's what they are," Cheyenne noted. "Although, I knew Brendon was up to something. He's a crappy liar."

The women laughed at that.

"Braydon, too," Jessie agreed. "But whenever I pushed, he changed the subject. To sex, of course."

More laughter.

"They're good at that, aren't they?" Kylie said.

"Too good," Cheyenne answered.

Bristol had known when she agreed to come that she would be one of the only single women there, and she hadn't been wrong. Then again, most of the time she was the only single one. Since she spent most of her free time with her best friend, Bianca, who was celebrating five years of wedded bliss, or with Rex, who'd recently pledged his life and love to Jack, or the Walkers, who were all celebrating wedded bliss, her relationship status tended to be at the forefront of her mind.

"I heard a rumor that the mayor's thinkin' about havin' a Valentine's Day auction next year." Kylie's eyes shifted to Bristol. "Since she's your best friend, do you know anything about that?"

"It's more than a rumor," she agreed. "And it's only one of many events she's got planned for next year."

"Yeah? She raisin' money for somethin'?" Cheyenne inquired.

Bristol nodded. "She's got a list and it gets longer every day."

"Bianca's good in that role," Jessie said. "And she's doin' a good job raising money. The fall festival was better than ever this year. I heard she raised enough to ensure every resident had a Thanksgiving meal."

Bristol nodded again. "She did. But she had a lot of help."

"That's right," Cheyenne said. "Lorrie headed up the committee, didn't she?"

"She most certainly did." Bristol smiled at the memory. Lorrie was a force to be reckoned with, and the woman didn't know the meaning of half-ass.

Which explained where her boys got it from.

"What's she gonna auction?" Zoey asked.

"Single men," Bristol blurted and felt her face heat from embarrassment.

"Seriously?" Kylie sat up, eyes wide. "That's a brilliant idea."

Jessie laughed. "I agree. Can you imagine?"

Bristol didn't bother to mention that she'd been tasked with finding the men who would fill the ten open spots Bianca had.

"You know who'd be perfect to auction off?" Cheyenne said. "Those two."

Glancing in the direction Cheyenne motioned with her chin, Bristol noticed Kaden and Keegan talking to Mack at the bar. She watched them for a moment, tried to envision a horde of women bidding on a single date with one or both of them. It wasn't hard to visualize, but for some reason, she wasn't excited about the idea.

"I'm gonna get us another round," Jessie said, getting to her feet.

"I'd bet they'd get the highest bid," Kylie said when her sister walked away.

"Agree," Zoey stated. "Although, there're quite a few single men in this town."

"Would they go as a pair?" Cheyenne asked.

"Most definitely," Zoey answered. "Kaleb told me they have a pact. They plan to marry one woman, share her between them."

"Yeah, well, we all know pacts can be broken," Cheyenne said. "Most figured Braydon and Brendon would do the same."

"True, but I think it's different with them," Zoey said. "They've never dated separately."

"Seriously? Never?" Kylie whistled as she stared at the twins.

Bristol had heard that, too. And ever since Kaden and Keegan had come to town years ago, she'd never seen them apart. It was as though they were connected at the hip.

"You gonna bid on them?"

Bristol's head swiveled toward Kylie as the softly spoken words registered. "Me?"

Kylie grinned.

"Oh, no. Totally not my thing."

"What's not your thing?" Jessie asked, setting three drinks on the table. "Hold that thought. I'll be right back."

When she returned with the last two, Jessie took a seat and kept her eyes on Bristol, eyebrows raising as though she was ready for an answer.

"We were talkin' about Kaden and Keegan," she informed her. "How they share their women."

Jessie glanced over her shoulder at the twins, then turned back.

"Well, all I have to say is don't knock it till you've tried it," Kylie supplied. "Two men is ... quite interesting."

The women laughed even as Bristol's face heated once again.

Chapter Six

CURTIS WALKER SAT IN THE LEATHER CHAIR, watching as his grandkids—those old enough to walk, anyway—got in line to meet and greet Santa Claus. It was utter chaos. A lot of chattering, a few giggles, plenty of distraction, and even a couple of tears.

Even in this grand hotel, Curtis felt right at home, but he figured his boys had known he would when they came up with the idea of a Christmas getaway. They'd certainly gone out of their way to make the environment comfortable. Homey, even. He doubted this place saw this sort of action on a good night. While he'd never inquired what went on here—didn't need to know— Curtis couldn't help but wonder if this place had ever seen a kid before this event.

No, he doubted it. Hell, it probably hadn't seen this many clothes, either.

Not that Curtis had come to the hotel since it had opened its doors to those who were lucky enough to get an invitation, nor had his boys made the offer. And while he wasn't exactly comfortable with the nature of this resort, he was proud of his boys for what they'd created. Their success was all he cared about, and even when he wasn't necessarily behind the concept of public debauchery, he would never hold back his approval for their desire to succeed.

His attention shifted to the heavyset man heading over to the enormous chair that had been set up, decorated with a backdrop that did a damn fine job of resembling the North Pole from the many fiction books his grandkids favored.

"Ho, ho, ho," the man bellowed heartily, smiling at the kids as he rested a hand on his big, round belly.

Curtis wasn't sure who the guy was, but he had to admit, the man was the spitting image of ol' St. Nick, right down to the jolly eyes and jelly belly. Curtis figured Travis had found the best of the best and was sparing no expense by giving the kids a last-minute chance to tell the man in the suit what they wanted for Christmas. He remembered doing the same for his boys growing up, though they'd used the chimney-sweeping old man as a means of keeping their boys in line. They didn't have any of the creepy elf things that sat on the shelf and stared eerily over the household. Oh, no. They'd threatened that Santa wouldn't be stopping by. For the most part, it had worked.

"Hey, Pop. Would you mind holdin' her?"

Curtis drew his attention away from the white-bearded man to Ethan as he stepped closer, five-month-old Kiera in his arms.

Mind? He would be delighted.

"Come here, darlin'," Curtis said, extending his arms. "Don't like Santa much, huh?"

"That's an understatement," Ethan muttered, passing her over. "I'll be back in a few. Gonna help Beau with the boys."

"Take your time," he told the boy. "We'll be fine right here, won't we, baby girl?"

When Kiera settled in his arms, she laid her head on his chest, and Curtis exhaled with a smile on his face. He held her as he'd done a few dozen times, watching the other little ones getting ready to have their pictures snapped, not realizing this event was as much for the parents' memories as for the kids' enjoyment. Curtis knew Lorrie had dozens of snapshots of their boys with Santa over the years. And they weren't just on paper anymore. Last year, with the help of his daughters-in-law, Lorrie had converted them to digital, or so she'd told him. But he didn't need a computer to remember what had been frozen in time. Some where they were smiling, others where they were bawling and desperate to get away, even a few when they were teeny tiny and sleeping in the bearded man's arms.

"Probably should've had them take naps before they did this," Lorrie said when she came over, her beautiful face alight with happiness as she cradled the newest member of their family to her chest. Only a few weeks old, Dustin was sleeping through the festivities, but still part of the action.

This was exactly where his bride of more than fifty years wanted to be, surrounded by family, their grandbabies with them. Didn't matter the holiday—birthdays, Christmas, Easter, Fourth of July, even St. Patrick's Day—these instances were what she looked forward to most. And as long as she was happy, Curtis was happy.

"Best to get it over with early," he told her.

"Yes. Especially since Travis has been holding out on the snow machine."

Curtis chuckled. "Using it as leverage to keep them in line?"

"Of course."

He glanced over at his oldest boy. Travis looked happy as he stood with his arm over Kylie's shoulder, the other holding Maddox. Gage was attempting to corral the other kids in line. No sooner would he get one settled than another would pop out of line and wander elsewhere.

One step forward, two steps back, that was the way it was with little ones.

"I still can't believe he did this," Lorrie said softly. "It's wonderful."

Curtis knew she wasn't referring to Santa or the snow machine or the many other activities the kids had undergone since their arrival yesterday. No, Lorrie was referring to the fact their boys had understood what Lorrie had worked hard to instill in them since they were little. Family was everything, and now that they were married and settled down, they were carrying on the tradition. One day, the grandbabies would be doing the same.

If for no other reason than that, Curtis couldn't help thinking they'd succeeded at this parenting thing.

MACK WAS DAMN GLAD THEY HADN'T ASKED him to play Santa Claus. Oh, he'd done it before. Reluctantly, of course. Years and years ago at his wife's insistence, back when Daniel was a baby, he'd donned the red suit and cheap white beard in an effort to impress his kid. Even though Daniel had been beside himself with glee, Mack had hated every second of it.

Story of his life, it seemed. The more he hated his own existence, the happier Daniel seemed to be.

"Hey, Mack."

Mack turned to see Curtis motioning toward the chair beside him. The very one Lorrie had just vacated. She offered him a smile and a pat on the shoulder as she passed.

"Take a load off, boy."

He smiled, more so at the man referring to him as a boy. Mack hadn't been a boy in a long-ass time. In fact, he would be celebrating his fifty-seventh birthday in less than two weeks. Something he preferred not to think about.

"How's your brother doin'?" Curtis asked when Mack settled into the chair.

"He's good," Mack told him. "Spendin' Christmas with his wife on a Caribbean island."

Curtis laughed. "Robert always was the adventurous one, wasn't he?"

That was an understatement. And at sixty, the man acted as though he was still in his twenties. But he was happy. Genuinely.

"How's the bar treatin' you?" Curtis inquired.

Unable to look the man in the eye, Mack nodded. "Good."

"I heard a rumor you're thinkin' about sellin'."

Mack sighed. "Just a rumor."

"Glad to hear that. Not sure what this town'd be without Moonshiners."

Unfortunately, they'd likely figure that out soon enough. Unless, of course, the new owners decided to keep the name.

Watching the kids take turns talking to Santa, Mack tried not to think about it. Didn't work. Every time he considered following through with Daniel's request, his stomach twisted in knots. Moonshiners had once belonged to his brother, Robert, and Mack had come to think of it as their family legacy. Not that the place made much money, but it did enough to keep shelter over his head and food in his belly. These days, those were the only things he cared about anyway.

His attention was still lingering on the Santa setup, though he wasn't seeing much of anything when he heard the familiar voice. It drew him out of his mind-wandering episode and back to the present.

"Sheriff," Curtis greeted, getting to his feet, shifting his granddaughter easily, never interrupting her afternoon snooze. "Good to see you."

The two men shook hands, as was customary for men in this town. Didn't matter that Curtis and Jeff were related by the marriage of their children, they still showed one another the respect they deserved.

"I was just about to head upstairs," Curtis stated. "Figured this one could use a little quiet."

Curtis peered down at him and Mack met the other man's steel-blue gaze. He didn't have to be good at reading people to see what the eldest Walker was doing.

"Take my seat, Jeff. Help Mack keep an eye on those rug rats."

Jeff chuckled, though he didn't look at Mack. "It'd be my pleasure."

"I'll talk to you later, boy," Curtis said, meeting Mack's stare and offering a knowing smile.

"Yes, sir," he said politely, even though he'd recognized the old bait-and-switch routine.

"Looks like they've got it all under control," Jeff said as he took a seat.

"Looks like," Mack muttered, unable to look at him.

"Town's quiet this mornin'."

"That's good."

"Hopin' it'll stay that way through tomorrow."

"Yep," Mack said, still unable to look at Jeff.

"How's Daniel?"

"Good."

"He here?"

"In Austin with his mama."

"You gonna see him for Christmas?"

Since the questions seemed to be getting more personal, Mack forced his gaze to settle on Jeff. The moment their eyes met, that weird churning in his stomach returned. It was a combination of nerves and regret. Every time he looked at Jeff, he was reminded of all that he'd lost. Well, technically, all that he'd thrown away, because it had been his choice to call a halt to their relationship.

"Probably not," he replied.

Jeff nodded, as though the answer made sense.

"Look, I only came because Travis invited me," Mack explained, keeping his voice low. "I'm not here to make it weird."

"But it is," Jeff said simply, as though he accepted it.

And he was right, it was definitely awkward. Almost as though not a single day had passed since Mack had forced himself to walk away from the only man he'd ever loved with everything he was. Still did, too. In fact, Mack had vowed he would never take another lover for the rest of his days because there was only one he wanted, one he couldn't have.

He'd figured that was a decent penance for hurting Jeff by ending their relationship. Only, he knew Jeff had remained single as well. Every time the sheriff's name was brought up in conversation, Mack feared he would hear how he'd found someone, was moving on with his life. The pain the thought inflicted was unbearable, but he knew that was him being selfish.

When the constriction shifted to his chest, Mack got to his feet. "I should go."

In an instant, Jeff was standing before him, stepping in close. "You could, but that won't change a damn thing."

Mack's eyes widened at the tortured note in Jeff's voice.

"We're gonna hash this out. Sooner or later." There was a promise in Jeff's softly spoken words. "You can only run for so long."

He wanted to argue that he hadn't been running, but Mack knew it was futile. Although he'd remained in place, he had been separating himself from everyone in this town. Hell, from the town itself and it was killing him.

"There's nothin' to hash out," Mack finally said when it was clear Jeff was waiting for him to say something.

"See, that's where you're wrong. There's plenty." The man stepped in closer. "And mark my words, we will finish this. One way or the other."

With that, Jeff walked away.

Once again, Mack's heart followed.

Chapter Seven

"AND SHE'S FINALLY DOWN FOR THE COUNT," Beau whispered when he stepped away from Kiera's portable crib, a smile on his sexy mouth.

Beau glanced at his watch.

"I think it's a record, too. Your dad said she took a two-hour nap earlier."

Yep, that was what Pop had said.

As though he was nervous, Beau walked over to the dresser, began rearranging things on top of it. There was baby shit strewn across the room. Bottles, pacifiers, toys, blankets, diapers. Everything they had at home had been relocated here, as though they were staying for a month, not a few days. Of course, having it there made Ethan feel better because he knew the kids wouldn't need anything. It was still endearing to watch his husband fret over which things to take and ultimately deciding on everything.

Ethan watched Beau, unable to hide his desire for the man.

Pushing up from the edge of the bed, he reached for Beau's hand. "Now that they're asleep, we should commence with the festivities."

"Festivities?" Beau whispered, clearly not wanting to wake the sleeping babies.

Without responding, Ethan tugged Beau's arm, leading the way to the monstrous bathroom attached to the fancy room. He snagged the baby monitor from the dresser before stepping inside and closing the door behind them, ensuring it didn't click. The triplets were light sleepers, and they'd learned even the softest sound seemed to wake them.

"Did you lock the door?" Beau asked.

"Yes," Ethan assured him. "Even put on the privacy latch."

Beau nodded, though he still seemed nervous.

Ethan set the monitor on the vanity, then stepped over to the shower and flipped on the water. When he turned back to Beau, the man was already removing his shirt, revealing his enormous chest. Ethan smiled but stopped Beau's hand before he could undo the button on his jeans.

"Relax. Let me take care of you," he whispered, closing the distance between them. "This is my present to unwrap."

"It most certainly is," Beau agreed, cupping Ethan's face and pulling him in for a kiss.

Their lips fused together, a soft mating at first. Ethan was in no hurry, wanting to savor this moment with his man. More importantly, he wanted Beau to chill. He was strung tight, likely in protective dad mode since they weren't safely ensconced in their house.

He backed Beau against the door and leaned into him, their tongues mating as Ethan's hands roamed freely over Beau's chest, his stomach, and finally around to his back. He devoured him slowly as the steam from the shower began to fill the space. By the time he pulled back, they were both breathing hard.

As he stared into Beau's beautiful brown eyes, Ethan released the button on Beau's jeans, slowly inched the zipper down. His husband's chest rose and fell rapidly, his stomach muscles tightening against Ethan's knuckles. And when he hooked his fingers and dragged the denim down Beau's long legs, his husband let out a sigh.

God, he loved this man, and it amazed him that the love he had for him seemed to grow more and more every minute of every day. Every time he saw Beau with one of their babies, that love grew tenfold. There was no denying Beau was the best father to have ever graced the earth, and with him, Ethan was a better man.

"Please, E."

Ethan eased to his knees, the hard tile of the floor beneath him, the sexy man before him. He smiled up at Beau as he fisted his cock, stroking slowly, reverently. He had no desire to rush this, though he wasn't sure Beau was going to appreciate his need to linger. His husband looked to be strung tight already, and Ethan hadn't even taken him in his mouth yet.

Granted, he changed that instantly, sliding his tongue over the swollen head.

Beau hissed, his head dropping back against the door as his hips shifted forward.

"Look at me," Ethan whispered. "Watch me."

Though his head looked too heavy for his neck to hold up, Beau did as he was instructed, his heavy-lidded eyes coming to rest on Ethan's face.

Only then did Ethan take him in his mouth, sucking him deep and slow, curling his tongue around the thick shaft. Ethan moaned when Beau's fingers twined in his hair. He wasn't controlling him, simply touching.

"I love you, E," Beau said softly.

Ethan didn't respond with words. Instead, he laved Beau's rigid cock with his tongue, sliding over the sensitive underside, then lower. He teased Beau's balls with his tongue and lips before sucking his heavy sac in his mouth, fondling him gently. His own cock was straining against his zipper, desperate to be inside this man.

"I don't wanna come yet," Beau warned. "I want you inside me when I do."

A deep growl escaped Ethan, but he didn't stop his ministrations, continuing to love Beau slowly, paying attention to every detail, ensuring he pushed every single one of Beau's buttons.

He pulled back temporarily. "Fuck my mouth. Then I'll take your ass."

Beau's eyes flared with heat as his other hand shifted, curling around Ethan's chin. The big man held his head in place as he rocked his hips forward and back, driving deep into Ethan's throat, accepting what Ethan was willing to give him. Long minutes passed as Beau's soft moans drifted on the humid air. Ethan's body hardened as Beau's cock pulsed against his tongue. He was close. So damn close, and it required effort to keep from pushing his husband over that slippery edge.

Suddenly, Beau hissed and pulled back, panting as he slumped against the wall.

Ethan chuckled, loving how easily he could push Beau to the brink.

He got to his feet, then shed his own clothes while Beau kicked off his jeans. A minute later, they were in the shower. This time Ethan was pressed into the wall, Beau's heavy weight pinning him there as their tongues explored.

"Inside me, E," Beau pleaded.

"My pleasure, baby."

Ethan snagged the bottle of lube he'd stashed in here for exactly this reason. While Beau stood beneath the spray, the water dripping down his hard body, Ethan stroked himself firmly, slicking his cock as he ached to get inside the man.

"Turn around," Ethan ordered, his words clipped, a burning need pulling at his self-control.

Beau pivoted, planted his hands on the tile, and leaned forward.

Stepping behind him, Ethan slid his cock along the crack of Beau's ass, enjoying the urgent pleas that became a constant as Beau's need reached a crescendo.

Rather than impale him, Ethan inched inside Beau's tight ass slowly, retreating nearly all the way, then pushing in deeper. His cock throbbed with the need for release because it had been days since he'd felt the blessed heat of Beau enveloping him. Somehow Ethan managed to hold on, thrusting his hips forward until he was fucking him ruthlessly.

"E … oh, fuck … don't stop." The words were raspy and soft but no less potent.

Ethan gritted his teeth as unbelievable pleasure consumed him, every nerve in his body singing as he fucked the man he loved more than life. When he nearly came from the sensation, he reached around Beau, fisted his cock, and jerked him roughly.

Beau panted, mumbling his name over and over, begging for release until Ethan couldn't contain it any longer.

When he released Beau's cock, his husband's hand replaced his as Ethan gripped Beau's hips, holding on as he slammed into him. He waited until Beau groaned, his body jerking as he came.

When Ethan let go, he was pretty damn sure his head had blown clear off his body.

"ALL RIGHT, BOSS MAN, WHERE DO YOU want this stuff?" Kaleb asked when he joined Travis in the main floor recreation room.

"Under the tree," he told his brother. "Make sure all the packages are marked, though."

While his brothers carted down the gifts that had come from Santa, setting them up for the kids to find in the morning, Travis made his way to the kitchen, where Gage was putting together the cookies and milk that Kate had insisted they set out.

"There're some carrots in the fridge," Gage told him.

Ah, yes. Carrots for the reindeer, of course. The things their daughter came up with.

Travis retrieved the bag of baby carrots, then tossed them onto the stainless-steel counter beside Gage.

"You have to open them."

Travis did.

"Now you have to bite a couple, so it looks like the reindeer ate them."

"Why on earth would the reindeer be inside and leave the carrots behind?" Travis mused as he tore off the end of the bag and opened the resealable package.

"How're the kids gonna find them if we don't?"

True. Didn't mean it made any damn sense.

Since Travis didn't like carrots, he didn't bother biting them, just snagged a handful and tossed them on the plate Gage had sitting out.

"Please tell me those are chocolate chip," Sawyer said when he sauntered into the room.

"They are," Gage answered, then smacked Travis's hand when he reached for one.

Sawyer chuckled.

"What time's Mom comin' down to start the turkey?" Ethan asked when he joined them.

"Early," Gage told him. "Kylie set her alarm for four, so I figure sometime around then."

Zane groaned, walking in. "I am *not* gettin' up at four."

Maybe not, but Travis figured Reid—Zane's oldest—would be. Right alongside Kate, who would be coming down to pillage what Santa had brought her. You had to love kids and their excitement.

"Me, neither," Brendon added.

Travis hopped up on the counter, watched as the rest of his brothers stepped into the kitchen, circled the long counter where Gage was setting the last pan of cookies.

"We can eat them all, right?" Braydon asked, earning a slap from Gage, too.

"You have to leave a couple," Gage told them.

Travis knew his husband hadn't baked two dozen cookies for them to leave out for Santa. He'd made two dozen so they could leave one behind, along with some crumbs. It was their tradition at home and he'd insisted on doing the same here. Granted, they generally shared the cookies with the kids before they went to bed, stored a dozen for later, but tonight they were sharing with his brothers.

As Braydon and Brendon ribbed one another about who usually ate all the cookies, Travis smiled.

While the past two days had been hectic, to say the least, it had been worth every chaotic minute. And tomorrow morning, when all those kids woke to find presents under the tree from Santa … that would be the icing on the cake.

"How about some eggnog?" Zane asked, marching toward the industrial refrigerator.

"I'll get the bourbon," Sawyer offered, heading out to the bar.

"Make mine a double," Travis told him when he returned. "Without the eggnog."

Sawyer smirked. "Great minds…"

After eight drinks were made, two without the nasty shit, Travis lifted his glass. "To a new tradition."

"You plannin' to do this again next year?" Sawyer asked, eyes wide.

"And the year after that," Travis replied.

"That's a great idea," Zane offered.

"To a new tradition, then," Braydon stated, lifting his glass.

His brothers grinned wide and echoed the sentiment. They clinked glasses, then resumed conversations while they munched on chocolate chip cookies and bourbon. Zane was the one to gnaw the ends off a couple of carrots, Brendon doing the honors of chugging down half a glass of milk. Before they managed to get sloppy drunk, Gage reined them in, leading the way back to the tree.

Travis relocated a small table so Gage could set up the plate, the glass, the remnants of Santa's midnight feast.

Then they toasted once more to the best Christmas ever before heading off to bed. After all, four o'clock would come early for the women who insisted on making the Christmas feast. And Travis knew it wouldn't be long after that Kate would be insisting they come down to see what Santa had left.

Despite the fact he was exhausted, Travis found he couldn't wait for morning, either, just so he could see the smiles on his kids' faces.

Chapter Eight

Wednesday, December 25, 2019

AS FAR AS LORRIE WAS CONCERNED, CHRISTMAS was her favorite holiday. For more reasons than the obvious, though that was equally important.

Still, this was the day she looked forward to spending with her family. As many as they could fit in one space. This year they were blessed because the idea to gather at her boys' resort allowed for far more than would fit in her house.

The past couple of days had been amazing, but today was the real treat because her brothers and two of her sisters had been able to be there, along with a handful of their grown children. Curtis's brothers and sisters had managed to make it as well, along with some of their adult children. Add in Lorrie's seven sons, two sons-in-law, six daughters-in-law, three granddaughters, and twenty grandsons, and they had the makings of a party of epic proportions.

Now that the Christmas presents had been opened, Santa's gifts as well, they were all sitting down to a lunch feast that had taken roughly eight hours to prepare. Luckily, they'd had the use of a commercial kitchen; otherwise, Lorrie wasn't sure they would've been able to handle it all. Thanks to that and all the extra hands, it had turned out far better than expected. And the good news was, there would be plenty of leftovers for later this evening when everyone wandered back for more.

Now as she sat at a table with Curtis, she couldn't help but smile at all the faces. There were dozens of conversations taking place at the many tables scattered throughout the restaurant, and everyone seemed to be enjoying themselves.

"You all right, darlin'?" Curtis asked, leaning over and whispering in her ear.

"Better than," she assured him.

"Can I get you anything?"

"I'm good for now, thank you."

He pressed a kiss to her cheek, then turned his attention back to Gerald, who was sitting on his other side.

Lorrie looked around, caught sight of Travis laughing at something Gage said, Kylie smiling at Kate, who was telling a story, based on her animated hand gestures.

There was Kaleb offering Zoey a bite of the cornbread dressing while she blushed like a school girl.

Zane was holding Dustin in his arms, giving V a chance to eat before he did.

Ethan and Beau were focused on the triplets in their high chairs.

Brendon and Braydon were completing one another's sentences, though Lorrie couldn't hear the conversation.

And Sawyer was making an airplane motion with a spoon, delivering food to Matthew, while Brody stared wide-eyed at his father.

It was a perfect gathering.

Then again, it would've been perfect if they'd burned the pies or overcooked the turkey. None of that mattered in the grand scheme of things, because her family had long ago learned to overcome the small things because they had one another.

And that was a gift that kept on giving, year after year.

IT HAD BEEN A HECTIC DAY, BUT a damn good one, Mack thought.

First the kids storming the Christmas tree, all that wrapping paper scattered everywhere, the adults attempting to corral two dozen kids and convince them it was okay to share their toys with their brothers, sisters, cousins, whatever. Then there'd been the incredible lunch, the afternoon crash from too much food, returning for more so they could once again overdo it. After that last meal, Mack had offered to help clean the mess, but Kennedy had ushered him right out, assuring him they had it covered.

Now that things had finally settled down, Mack made his way over to the makeshift bar he'd manned for the last couple of nights. It wasn't Moonshiners, but it was decent as far as temporary setups went. He was happy to see several people had come down, mostly men tonight. Kaleb and Ethan were sitting at a table putting together what looked like a Lego figure, probably something Kaleb had bought one of his boys. Sawyer and Brendon were giving the enormous tree a once-over, likely wondering if they could top it next year. He hoped all the moms were taking a load off now that the major festivities had ceased. Kids were probably playing with their shiny new toys in their hotel rooms, eyes getting heavy or closed altogether.

Mack had considered heading home rather than staying another night, but he'd changed his mind at the last minute. Not exactly sure why that was, though. After he'd gotten the third degree from Daniel via text message of all things, he knew he wouldn't be able to endure sitting alone with himself all night long. So, here he was.

As he reached for a bottle of bourbon, his attention was snagged by the handsome sheriff coming down the dramatic staircase.

Yeah, okay, so Jeff was the real reason he was still here.

He tried to be discreet as he took Jeff in from head to toe. Tonight he was wearing a navy blue button down with his Wranglers and boots. The sleeves were rolled up, revealing his ropey forearms, the top button opened at his throat. He looked good, but that wasn't anything new.

It didn't make sense that he'd hung around for this, even Mack could admit as much, but he'd wanted to have a few more minutes where he didn't have to worry about the outside world. More specifically, Daniel finding out that Mack was still holding a torch for Jeff. He'd done a damn good job of hiding it, or at least he hoped he had.

When Jeff made it to the bottom of the stairs, his eyes scanned the space, coming to rest on him. Mack instantly averted his eyes, but he figured it was too late. Jeff had busted him ogling him.

Oh, well.

"What can I get ya?" Mack offered Travis when the man sidled up to the bar.

"Just beer tonight."

Mack bent down and retrieved a bottle from the mini-fridge kept under the long wooden counter. Had they been at Moonshiners, he would've offered Travis what he had on draft, but this was clearly a temporary setup, so he made the best of what he had.

"Thanks," Travis said when Mack passed it over after removing the cap.

Jeff came over and took the stool beside Travis.

"I didn't get a chance to thank you for inviting me," Jeff told Travis.

"You're family," Travis countered. "No thanks necessary. Glad you could be here. How'd Matthew and Brody fare?"

Mack didn't bother asking what Jeff wanted, he poured two fingers of scotch, then passed over the glass.

Jeff's hazel eyes met his briefly and Mack felt the intensity.

"Very well," Jeff told Travis. "I'm not sure their bedrooms'll hold all the shit they acquired."

Unfortunately, Mack didn't have the responsibilities that tended to pull him away from the bar, so he found himself standing there, waiting for someone to ask for something. When no one appeared, he felt like an idiot. He would've been better off at home, drowning himself in whiskey, pretending his life hadn't gone to the shitter because of his own lack of backbone.

"I'm headin' out in the mornin'," Jeff told Travis. "Back to the grindstone for me."

Travis grinned. "You're gonna miss another day with the snow machine."

Jeff chuckled softly. "No offense, but I'd rather break up a brawl than get in the middle of that."

Thankfully, Kaden and Keegan appeared, giving Mack an excuse to walk away rather than ogle the sheriff any longer.

"You seen Bristol?" Kaden asked, his voice low as though he didn't want anyone to overhear. "She said she'd meet us down here."

"Not lately," Mack told him. "Can I get you somethin'?"

"What does Bristol normally drink?"

"Vodka and cranberry," Mack told him without missing a beat.

"We'll take the vodka," Keegan said. "If that's cool."

Mack glanced down the bar at Travis. When the man nodded, Mack snagged the Grey Goose from the top shelf, passed it over.

Without another word, the twins headed in the direction of the elevator.

"Hey, Mack."

He turned at the sound of Travis's voice, moved closer while doing his damnedest not to look at Jeff.

"In case I don't see you in the mornin', I wanted to thank you for comin'," Travis told him, holding out his hand.

Mack shook it. "Thanks for invitin' me."

"You're family, too. Don't ever forget that."

Mack nodded.

"All right, I'm headin' upstairs. Hopin' to get a few good hours of sleep tonight so we can do it all again tomorrow."

Mack offered a good night after Jeff did, then attempted to make a clean getaway. Before he could get out from behind the bar, Jeff's stern voice pulled him up short.

"We need to talk."

Mack stopped moving, took a deep breath to calm himself, then managed to redirect his feet. Swallowing hard, he made his way down to the end of the bar, where Jeff was still sitting. "What's on your mind?"

"Not here," Jeff told him as he got to his feet.

Before he could toss out an excuse, Mack glanced around, realizing he wasn't technically on duty. This was a help-yourself type of establishment, at least for the evening, so his expertise wasn't needed. Which meant he couldn't get out of this without looking like an ass.

In an effort to stall, Mack opened the refrigerator, grabbed a can of Coke, flipped the top, took a sip.

"Mack." Jeff's tone reflected his impatience.

He considered chugging the soda but figured he'd need it more once this conversation kicked off. His gaze swung to the bottle of Jack on the shelf. Perhaps he'd need that, too.

"Let's talk," Jeff stated again.

With a resigned sigh, Mack gripped his Coke and fell into step with Jeff. He didn't bother to ask where they were going or what they were going to talk about. It honestly didn't matter to him, because this was the very reason he was here, right? To steal those few extra minutes with this man. At some point, he figured Jeff was going to give him what for, considering the way he'd ended things. Since he deserved the sheriff's wrath, he figured tonight was as good as any.

When they stepped into the elevator, Jeff pushed a button, the doors closed. A minute later, they opened again and Mack's feet moved of their own volition, his legs carrying him wherever Jeff wanted to go.

The only time he paused was when Jeff scanned his key card and opened the hotel room door.

Jeff must've realized he was frozen because he turned back. "Come in, Michael."

Mack's heart thumped hard against his sternum. Jeff was the only one who ever called him that, and usually only when they'd been intimate.

With his heart in his throat, Mack stepped into the room with only one question on his mind: Was he about to do something they would both regret tomorrow?

JEFF ENDSLEY KNEW THIS WAS GOING TO backfire in a big fucking way, but he couldn't stop the train now that it was out of the depot. At some point, a derailment was inevitable, and he was smart enough to know that. Especially if things progressed the way he hoped they would.

But for the first time in years, he didn't give a shit about that, either.

When Mack finally stepped into the room, Jeff closed the door behind him, flipped the lock, though he doubted privacy was an issue right now. No one was going to come looking for either one of them tonight.

He hoped.

"What'd you wanna talk about?" Mack asked, his voice gruff as usual, his wary blue eyes scanning the room but never settling.

Figuring there was no sense in beating around the bush, Jeff walked up to Mack, took the can of Coke from his hand, and set it on the dresser. Mack's gaze followed the can, as though he worried what would happen to it.

Jeff knew better. Hell, he was an officer of the law, and he'd long ago learned how to read body language. Mack's was screaming *Run! Fast! While you still can.*

He didn't wait for Mack to turn around and look at him; instead, Jeff stepped up behind him. Their eyes met in the mirror over the dresser.

"What are you doin'?" Mack rasped, his eyes wide.

Jeff leaned in, allowed his lips to lightly graze Mack's ear while he still held his stare in the mirror. "What we've both wanted for so fucking long."

When Jeff nipped Mack's earlobe, the big man groaned softly, a sound he'd missed so damn much. It had been nearly five painfully long years since Mack had ended their relationship. And during that time, Jeff hadn't exactly pined away for the man, but he hadn't rushed to move on with his life, either.

Sliding his arms beneath Mack's, Jeff planted his palms flat against Mack's hard stomach. The man sucked in air, and that was like a body slam, hitting Jeff from all angles, his muscles tightening as though preparing for another blow.

"I shouldn't be here," Mack said, even as he tilted his head to the side.

"This is the only place you should be," Jeff countered. "Where you've always belonged."

And while he hadn't put up a fight when Mack called things off, he knew he had waited far too long to fight for what he wanted. Since that day, Jeff had always planned to launch an offensive, to get Mack back no matter what it took. The only reason he hadn't was because he respected Mack's relationship with Daniel, although he didn't agree with the way Daniel played his father.

"Jeff…"

He ran his hands up Mack's thick chest, loving the way the muscles beneath the soft cotton T-shirt flexed. Jeff pressed his lips to Mack's neck, nipped him with his teeth. Mack hissed and jerked, but he didn't pull away, which Jeff took as a good sign.

"We shouldn't…" Mack moaned softly.

Oh, they most definitely should.

Slowly, Jeff slid one hand down over Mack's stomach as he lifted his head and met Mack's stare in the mirror once more. He continued lower, pausing at the button on Mack's jeans.

"Tell me to stop," Jeff whispered. "Tell me to stop and I will."

Mack's breaths were choppy, and though his eyes revealed far more than the man probably wanted, he didn't say no.

Jeff unhooked the button on Mack's fly, causing his stomach muscles to flex beneath Jeff's palms.

"Tell me to continue," he urged, needing Mack to be here with him. A willing participant.

Mack didn't say a word, but his hand moved over Jeff's and he urged him without words.

"Tell me," Jeff insisted. "Tell me you want this, Michael."

"I want this," Mack groaned. "More than I want any fucking thing."

Jeff didn't realize until that moment how much he'd needed to hear that. To know that Mack hadn't walked away without looking back. Jeff knew for a fact that Mack hadn't been seeing anyone. Not since he called things off. And though Jeff had considered getting back into the dating scene, he always found a reason to put it off.

The reason being he was and would always be in love with this man. Nothing would change that.

Before he could lower the zipper on Mack's jeans, the man spun around. The move surprised him almost as much as Mack taking complete control. Jeff's back met the wall seconds before Mack's hard body pressed up against him.

"We both know this is stupid," Mack growled softly.

Jeff held his stare, didn't flinch.

"Fuck…" Mack said on a rough exhale, then slammed his mouth over his.

Jeff lost control then. His hands slid into Mack's hair, holding him in place as every ounce of need he'd harbored rushed to the surface. He pushed away from the wall, forcing Mack backward. Hands and mouths fumbled as they stumbled over to the bed. In a strange twist, Jeff ended up flat on his back, Mack over him. Not that he minded. In this position, Jeff managed to jerk Mack's shirt over his head, tossed it across the room. His palms slid over the soft hair on Mack's chest, desperate to touch every inch of him.

Mack returned the favor, ripping at the buttons on Jeff's shirt until the damn thing came open. Jeff hissed when Mack's warm hands landed on his bare skin, his mouth soon to follow.

Jeff palmed Mack's head as the man trailed blazing-hot kisses over his sensitive flesh, working lower. He wasn't taking his time, either, and for that, Jeff was grateful. He'd waited so long for this.

Time seemed to stand still and speed up all at once. Jeff's boots and jeans ended up on the floor, his boxers soon to follow as Mack ripped at his clothes with a desperation that Jeff hadn't seen in a long damn time. Even before things had gone sideways.

"Fuck!" Jeff's back bowed off the bed when Mack took his cock in his mouth.

Incoherent words fell from his lips as he rocked his hips, attempting to go deeper into the blistering heat of Mack's devilish mouth. He endured as long as he could before that telltale tingle ignited in his spine. A rough growl escaped him as he thrust his hands in Mack's hair, jerking him back. Using the grip he had, he pulled Mack forward, then flipped their positions. He gave as good as he got, tearing at Mack's clothes until the big man was laid out naked before him. That was when Jeff took what he'd craved, sucking the wide head of Mack's cock between his lips.

He worked him over good, relishing the desperate groans that escaped him. Jeff had fantasized about this more times than he could count. He figured it was only fair. Before Mack had abruptly called a halt to their relationship, their sex life had been off the charts. And he fucking missed this.

"Don't…" Mack groaned, his big body drawing tight. "Don't make me come yet."

Jeff slowed his ministrations, then released Mack's cock. He looked up the hard lines of Mack's body, meeting his gaze. What he saw sent a tremor down his spine. Mack was as out of control as he was. And while it should've occurred to him that this would end badly, it didn't. Not at that moment.

Within seconds, Jeff had procured the lube he'd brought with him, crawled back on the bed with Mack as he slicked his cock.

"How do you want it?" he asked, gripping his erection in his fist as he settled between Mack's legs.

Mack's ocean-blue gaze flashed with heat. "Hard."

When Mack pulled his knees toward his chest, Jeff aligned his cock with the tight entrance to Mack's body. A second later, he was driving into him. Deep, hard. He didn't give a quarter, unable to hold back even though he knew he should have.

Mack's head fell back, eyes closed, a satisfied cry escaping him.

"Look at me!" Jeff demanded, leaning over him.

As he stared down into Mack's face, those ocean-blue eyes opened, locked onto his face. And right then and there, Jeff took them to the highest peak, but he didn't allow Mack to go over. He planted his fists on either side of Mack's head and stared down at him as he impaled him, driving his hips forward, retreating slowly, driving home again. He continued that excruciatingly slow pace, giving Mack exactly what he'd asked for.

"You want to come?"

Mack growled low in his throat. "Yes."

Jeff considered that for a moment, continuing to slam into him, filling him completely, slowly pulling back.

"Tell me."

"I want to come," Mack hissed.

"Don't you dare touch yourself."

Mack's eyes flashed once more as Jeff leveraged himself up, using Mack's legs as a brace. He pounded into him, fast, hard, oh-so-fucking deep. They were racing up that slope once more, and Jeff never took his eyes off Mack's face. The man held out until he couldn't, and when Mack came, it was with Jeff's name on his lips.

That hoarse rasp sent Jeff careening into the ether.

Chapter Nine

KEEGAN GRINNED OVER AT HIS BROTHER AS he lifted his hand. "Last chance to back out."

He waited for Kaden to change his mind, something his twin was prone to do.

"She told us she'd meet us," Keegan reminded him. "True gentlemen will check on a lady, right?"

Before Kaden could say a word, Keegan dropped his knuckles to the door. Three quick raps and he was stepping back.

Kaden sighed. "She's probably as—"

The door opened and Bristol appeared, fresh-faced, her silky brown hair pulled back into her normal ponytail. Her eyebrows lowered, confusion written all over her beautiful face.

"Hey," she greeted even as she stuck her head out the door and peered down the hall. "What are you doing here?"

Keegan smirked. "The real question is why aren't you downstairs?"

Her eyes widened as though she just remembered she'd promised to meet them in the bar.

"I am so sorry. I must've forgotten."

Yep. Or she chickened out, which was likely her real reason for avoiding them.

"No worries. Mind if we come in?" Keegan asked, knowing his brother would be too tongue-tied to get the sentence out.

"In?"

Keegan held up the bottle of Goose, grinned. "Figured we'd bring the party to you. Hang out for a bit. Chat."

Bristol's eyes remained on his. "Chat?"

"Yeah. You know, that thing friends do?"

"Friends?"

Figuring they could spend half an hour doing this, Keegan took a step forward. "Perhaps we could have this discussion inside. Before we wake up any of those kiddos."

That seemed to get through to her, because Bristol took a step back, but she never took her eyes off them.

"I was getting ready for bed."

"Well, I was hopin' we could hang out," Keegan said, realizing Kaden really had lost the ability to speak.

Figured.

"And do what?" The edge of caution in Bristol's voice made him smile.

"Watch a movie? Play cards? Gossip? Doesn't matter," he told her, then held up the bottle. "As long as we come up with a way to finish off this bottle."

Bristol laughed and she seemed to settle somewhat. "Finish that off? It's not even open."

Keegan took care of that right quick. "Is now."

While Bristol and Kaden acted like teenagers who were forced to play seven minutes in heaven, Keegan made his way into the bathroom, retrieved the two glasses the hotel kept stashed there. Why *did* they put them in the bathroom, he wondered. Seemed an awkward place for glasses.

Not that it mattered.

"All right," he said when he returned. "You sit there." He motioned for Bristol to move to the bed. "You"—he pointed to Kaden—"can sit in that chair. And I'll take the floor."

"You're serious," Bristol said, but at least she was following directions, making her way over to the bed.

"Very. So what'll it be? Movie? Strip poker?" And because he'd thought of it and it sounded appealing, he added, "Seven minutes in heaven? We could play spin the bottle"—Keegan held up the bottle—"but we should probably wait till it's empty."

"I am not playing spin the bottle," Bristol said with a laugh.

"Seven minutes in heaven it is."

She laughed again and Keegan found he very much liked the sound. While he hadn't found himself quite as infatuated with the cute little daycare owner—not the way Kaden was, anyway—he certainly understood the appeal. When she wasn't on edge, she was fun and sweet and damn easy on the eyes.

Since neither of them had any suggestions, Keegan poured two fingers in each of the glasses, passed one to Bristol, the other to Kaden. Since he didn't have another, he figured he'd drink straight from the bottle.

No one spoke and Keegan realized it was going to get awkward really fast if he didn't do something.

"All right. Never have I ever, it is."

Bristol's cheeks turned a pretty shade of pink. "Seriously?"

"Yep. I assume you know how to play?"

She nodded. "Someone tells something they've never done before and anyone who has done it has to drink."

Keegan mock toasted her with the bottle. "You can go first."

"Me?"

Yep, he could totally understand why Kaden was head over heels for this chick. Seriously.

BRISTOL KNEW SHE SHOULDN'T HAVE ANSWERED THE door. She'd even considered it. It would've been easy to play it off tomorrow, to tell them she'd fallen asleep early, but her hand had turned that knob before her brain could get out the instruction.

And here she was, sitting in a semi-dark room with two of the sexiest men on the planet. She knew she would regret standing them up tonight, but she'd never anticipated they'd make a house call. Or hotel room, as was the case now.

Not that she had any intention of letting them know she wasn't entirely disappointed that they'd tracked her down. In fact, she planned to continue with the ruse of making them believe she had absolutely no interest. Which, of course, was a painful lie. But sometimes self-preservation was the most important thing.

"Should we put a time limit on this?" Keegan asked, a teasing note in his voice.

"I'm thinkin'," she argued, though she hadn't given a second's thought about something she'd never done.

Taking a deep breath, she willed her mind to quiet, to ignore the fact that Kaden and Keegan Walker had interrupted what would've been a perfectly boring night.

"Ten, nine…"

Bristol laughed. "Hush it. I'm thinkin'. Okay, fine. Never have I ever … stolen a car."

Keegan's sexy mouth curved into a wide grin while his twin's twitched. Kaden lifted his glass, drained it while Keegan took a swig on the bottle.

Bristol's eyes widened. "You've stolen a car?"

"Technically," Kaden said, "we misappropriated it. Temporarily."

Bristol raised her eyebrows, urging him to continue.

"It was our old man's car," Keegan explained. "Needless to say, we spent a good portion of our freshman year grounded."

Bristol realized she shouldn't have been surprised. Kaden and Keegan were the very definition of a bad boy. In duplicate.

"My turn," Keegan said. "Never have I ever snuck a boy in my bedroom window."

Realizing the twist he'd put on that, Bristol chuckled, only it came out as a snort. A very unladylike one, at that.

"Well?" Kaden prompted, his blue-gray eyes locked on her as though he couldn't wait to find out the answer.

Bristol took a big swallow of her drink.

"I knew it!" Keegan laughed. "Explain yourself, young lady."

"I was a junior, I think. His name was David. He was a senior and I thought he hung the moon."

"Did you get caught?" Kaden inquired.

"Nope. But I never did it again after that. I was so freaked out that my dad would catch me, I couldn't even look at him. He stayed for about twenty minutes, then hightailed it. Never talked to me again after that."

"Probably for the best," Keegan noted, then glanced at Kaden. "Your turn."

Kaden seemed to consider it, then said, "Never have I ever cried while watching a movie."

"Good one," Keegan said.

Bristol was the only one to drink.

"Last movie you cried at," Kaden prompted.

"Oh, geez." Bristol tried to think but wasn't even sure. "I have no idea, but I can admit, I tend to get weepy. I have no shame."

The game took off from there.

Bristol: "Never have I ever lied to get a job."

Kaden and Keegan both drank.

"Mechanic shop," Keegan supplied. "We were seventeen. Lied and said we were eighteen."

"Did you get hired?"

"Yep."

Keegan: "Never have I ever been on a fad diet."

Bristol drank, Kaden didn't.

"More than one," she admitted.

Kaden: "Never have I ever cut my own hair."

Keegan drank, Bristol did, too.

"I wanted bangs," Bristol said when Kaden stared at her. "For the record, it did not turn out well."

"Well, I shaved my head," Keegan admitted, getting to his knees to add more vodka to her glass.

"Did you do it, too?" she asked Kaden.

"Hell no. He looked like a douche."

That made her laugh so hard tears came to her eyes. It took a minute or two, but she finally calmed herself.

Bristol: "Never have I ever played strip poker."

"Totally missin' out, darlin'," Keegan said as he took a pull on the bottle.

Kaden downed his drink, held his glass out for more.

At this point, Bristol was feeling no pain, so she offered up her glass, too.

Keegan: "Never have I ever eaten food that fell on the floor."

Kaden drank, Bristol didn't.

"Five-second rule," Kaden said defensively, and followed it with a sinful smirk.

More vodka was added.

Kaden: "Never have I ever gotten a tattoo I regretted."

Keegan drank, Bristol didn't.

"I was drunk and stupid."

"What's the tattoo of?"

"An anchor." He tapped over his left shoulder to show where it was. "Luckily, I never have to look at it."

Bristol: "Never have I ever slept in the nude."

Both men drank. Kaden had to get more.

"Every night, darlin'," Kaden supplied.

Keegan: "Never have I ever regifted something someone gave me."

Bristol downed what was in her glass, laughing. She knew she should chill on the shots, but she couldn't seem to help herself. For the first time in a long time, she was totally chill.

"It gets worse," she explained, giggling. "It was a gift from Bianca. I gifted it back to her two years later. She totally busted me."

Both men laughed and she realized how much she loved the rough grind of their voices.

Keegan supplied more alcohol.

Kaden: "Never have I ever talked my way out of a ticket."

Bristol drank, Keegan didn't.

"I was sixteen," she told them. "And in my defense, I've never been pulled over since."

Another refill.

Bristol: "Never have I ever hated a gift but said I loved it."

Both men looked at one another, then drank.

"Our mother buys us socks for Christmas every year," Kaden noted.

Keegan: "Never have I ever tried to make someone jealous."

Bristol grinned, drank, and so did Kaden.

"That same guy in high school," she told them. "David."

"Did it work?"

She grinned at the memory. "Nope. But I figure that was my good fortune. He's been married three times now."

Kaden: "Never have I—"

"Okay," Bristol interrupted. "One more, then I have to stop or I'll be sick."

"Party pooper," Keegan teased as he poured a small amount in her glass.

Kaden: "Never have I ever wanted to date two men at one time."

Bristol's head was spinning from the alcohol. She blamed that for why she downed her drink. Luckily, their wide eyes stopped her from blurting exactly *who* she'd wanted to date at the same time.

Of course, Keegan didn't let it go.

"Spill it," he insisted.

She shook her head.

He was smiling as he got to his feet, moved over to the bed.

Bristol's lungs stopped working as she stared up at the handsome man. He was tall and lean and so freaking beautiful.

"Okay, give me a hint," he urged.

No way could she tell them. No freaking way.

"How old were you when you wanted to date two men at one time?" Kaden asked, joining his brother, both of them looming over her.

Bristol shook her head again. If she told them…

"Do I need to tickle it out of you?" Keegan's barely disguised threat made her laugh.

"Not ticklish," she told him. Luckily, it was true.

Evidently he didn't believe her, because Keegan took her empty glass, set it on the nightstand, then put one knee on the bed as he reached for her.

When his hand gripped her side, she couldn't have laughed if she'd wanted to. The air in the room became scarce, and a fierce heat took up residence inside her, flooding her veins. That was when she realized neither of them were laughing. Something had shifted in the air, taking their carefree game and turning it into something far more dangerous.

"Tell me somethin'," Keegan whispered, his eyes imploring her.

"Hmm?"

"Have you ever kissed twins?"

"No."

"Do you want to?"

His warm hand was still on her side, even though he kept a decent distance between them.

Bristol looked over at Kaden, held his gaze for a second, then revealed the one secret she'd sworn she would take to her grave.

KADEN HAD KNOWN THE SECOND KEEGAN SUGGESTED they pay Bristol a visit that there was a good chance things were going to get out of control. He'd been doubly certain of that when Keegan procured the vodka.

Then again, out of control was the name of the game when Keegan was in charge, and no doubt about it, his twin had taken the reins from the moment he knocked on her door.

His lungs were constricted as he waited with bated breath for her to answer Keegan's question of whether or not she wanted to slide down the slippery slope and kiss the two of them, to try some twin action on for size.

"Yes," Bristol whispered. "I do."

He was pretty damn sure his heart skipped a few beats as soon as those words tumbled out of her sweet, pouty lips.

Blame it on the alcohol or the game or, hell, on the setting, didn't matter. While Kaden was usually the level-headed one, he found himself doing something he never would've done had they not been in this particular room, with this particular woman.

Kaden put one knee on the bed, then leaned over Bristol, shouldering Keegan out of the way in the process. His brother was not about to sample the goods before him, because Christ Almighty, Kaden had been waiting too long for this.

He held Bristol's gaze as he got closer, waited for her to throw up the big red stop sign. That was the only reason he nearly fell over when Bristol reached for him, her soft, smooth fingers curling around his neck as she pulled him down until their mouths touched. His lips brushed hers ever so lightly, then more insistently. His tongue got with the program, sliding over her bottom lip. They shared air for a moment, and when she sighed, Kaden sealed his mouth to hers, kissing her the way he'd fantasized for months. Her soft moan reverberated against his lips, and it took tremendous effort not to press her into the mattress.

When he pulled back, he watched as her eyes slowly opened, glittering with a heat he'd only caught glimpses of before.

"My turn."

His brother's raspy words pulled him back from the edge. Rather than get up, though, Kaden drew his other leg up on the bed and shifted to the side, watching as Bristol locked lips with his twin.

Most people wouldn't understand their desire to share a woman between them, but that was the only thing they'd ever wanted. Hell, sometimes Kaden couldn't wrap his head around how it had come to be, but he'd long ago stopped trying to figure it out because this … here … with Bristol…

This was fucking perfect.

More so than any other moment in Kaden's entire existence.

Keegan growled low in his throat as he leaned over her. Bristol's hand remained curled around Keegan's neck, and she was pulling him down as she leaned back on the pillow. Kaden knew he should put a stop to this. Come tomorrow, when the three of them were battling hangovers, he damn sure didn't want regret to intrude, and there was no doubt in his mind that would happen. For Bristol, of course. Kaden wasn't going to regret a thing, unless, of course, he managed to push her away with this little stunt. While he'd suspected she was interested in them, Kaden had noticed she did her best to pretend otherwise.

He was just about to call a halt when Keegan's hand locked onto Kaden's wrist. His twin relocated his hand, setting it on Bristol's thigh before Keegan refocused on the kiss.

Bristol didn't push his hand away, even as he slid his palm down her shin until he reached her ankle. He caressed her smooth skin, working his way up her calf, pushing the thin pajama pants upward. He wasn't working to get them off her, merely wanted to touch, to explore. She was definitely as soft as he'd imagined, maybe softer.

God, he'd wanted this for so damn long. Wanted her.

Bristol moaned again, drawing Kaden's attention to the way her lips were still fused to Keegan's. Kaden didn't move, didn't interrupt, though he wanted to feel her mouth on his more than he wanted oxygen. He mimicked a statue, right up until she reached for him, her fingers gliding over his wrist. When she tugged, evidently wanting him closer, Kaden shifted, his thigh brushing hers. It was then she pulled back from Keegan.

Again, he waited for her to stop, but she surprised him, reaching for him.

Kaden had always prided himself on his self-control, but when it came to Bristol, it seemed to fail him. Epically. As his lips covered hers once more, he knew he needed to back off. The vodka had lowered her inhibitions, and if they moved forward, she would hate them both come morning.

And Kaden wasn't willing to risk that.

"God, you're sweet," he whispered, pulling his mouth back and pressing his forehead to hers. "So fucking sweet, Bristol."

She was breathing hard, as was he, more so when her hand slid beneath his shirt, her cool fingers brushing against his abs. Fucking hell.

This had to stop.

Kaden took a deep breath, reached for her wrist, and removed her hand, though it pained him to do so.

"You're gonna leave, aren't you?" she asked, her voice so soft he barely heard her.

"We are, yes. But when you're ready … *really* ready, Bristol … just know we're waitin' for you." Kaden lifted his head, met and held her gaze. "Only you."

He could see the hint of uncertainty in her eyes, but Kaden knew this was the only option. Falling into bed with her would be amazing. They could rock her world all fucking night long, but Kaden wanted a hell of a lot more than one night with her.

Forcing himself to his feet, Kaden met Keegan's eyes. His twin nodded once. They were on the same page, thank God.

"Dream about us," Keegan said softly, smiling down at her.

When Kaden stepped out into the hallway, his body ached with the need for her, but he was getting used to it. As it was, he'd wanted Bristol for so long, he wasn't sure he remembered a time when he wasn't aching for her.

"She's gonna push us away," Keegan said, lifting the vodka bottle to his lips as they headed toward the elevator to their floor.

"She is," he agreed, but all good things came to those who waited.

And Kaden was willing to wait as long as it took, because in the end, it would be so fucking worth it.

Chapter Ten

Saturday, December 28, 2019

FINALLY BACK HOME, THE KIDS TUCKED INTO their beds, Travis sat on the couch, Kylie curled up against him. As he stared at the television screen, his mind flipped through the images from the past week. The laughter, the smiles. It had turned out exactly as he'd hoped it would, the perfect Christmas gift.

"What's on your mind?" Kylie asked, turning her head so she was looking up at him.

Travis peered down at her. "Our vacation."

Her hand flattened over his chest, rubbing gently. "It was perfect, Travis. The kids had the best time."

"What about you?" He'd seen her smile, watched her laugh and interact with his family and hers, so he hoped she had enjoyed herself, though he honestly wasn't sure if he'd stopped long enough to ask.

"It was amazing. But I would've had a good time if we'd stayed here."

He kissed her forehead. "Really?"

"Yes. Anywhere is perfect, as long as you and Gage are with me, and the kids. I don't need much more than that."

"So that's a no to making it a yearly occurrence?"

Kylie giggled. "Hey, if you want all of us to invade the resort for five days out of every year, who am I to argue?"

"And the others? Did they have a good time?" Travis knew his insecurities were showing, but when it came to Kylie, he didn't care. She and Gage were the only two he allowed to see them, because he'd long ago accepted they would love him despite his flaws.

"From what I gathered, everyone's hoping for a repeat next year."

He nodded, glanced at the television.

"Only next year," she continued, "maybe we can be in on the secret. Help out some."

"You do enough as it is," he told her, pulling her closer to him.

"So do you," she countered, shifting so that she was sitting up.

Travis instantly missed her warmth, but he turned his full attention to her.

"Are you tellin' me you don't like surprises, wife?" he teased.

"Oh, I definitely like them." Kylie moved toward him, on her knees. "But I prefer to *give* them more than to get them."

When his wife straddled his thighs, he rested his hands on her hips. "Is that what you're doin' now?"

"Attempting to. Is it working?"

"Most definitely."

She leaned forward, smiled, then pressed her lips to his.

"You're gonna wake the beast," he informed her when she dipped her fingers into the waistband of his sweatpants.

"Does he want to come out and play?" she whispered, a teasing note in her voice.

"You know he does."

Kylie pressed her breasts to his chest, her other hand sliding down his whiskered jaw, his neck. Travis relaxed, letting her warmth consume him. He loved when his wife was playful like this. While he'd hoped to enjoy some stolen moments at the resort, time had gotten away from them these past few days. Mainly because they'd been stowed away with five little ones, and sneaking in some private time had been impossible.

"Do you think it's safe?" she asked, her lips gliding over his neck.

His response was a soft growl of approval as he pulled her hips forward, showing her how much he believed it was.

She was wearing one of Gage's T-shirts, and Travis loved how her scent mixed with Gage's. It went right to his head every damn time.

Sliding his hands back, he shifted his fingers so they were beneath the hem of the T-shirt, where it rested on her thighs. He inched upward as she continued to rain kisses on his neck.

"You're a dirty girl, Mrs. Walker," he whispered when he realized she wasn't wearing panties.

"It's your fault, Mr. Walker."

The sound of a throat clearing made Travis smile, but he didn't turn his head to look at Gage. "Join us," he insisted.

"Don't mind if I do," he said softly, coming to stand behind the couch, at Travis's back.

Kylie pulled back, and Travis knew she was watching Gage.

His husband's warm hand curled around his neck, massaging gently. Travis tilted his head forward, encouraging Gage to touch.

"Mmm. I like where this is headed," their wife said, giggling softly.

Heat slammed into Travis when he realized Gage had freed his cock from his jeans and Kylie was taking him in her mouth. His vision was restricted because she was on his lap, but he didn't need eyes. The sounds of her mouth working Gage over were more than enough to entice him.

Instinct had him glancing at the stairs, ensuring there were no shorties headed their way. When he was satisfied the kids weren't going to interrupt, Travis reached between his body and Kylie's, pushing his sweatpants down. His wife knew exactly what he was doing, because she lifted up, gave him room to work as he forced the cotton down his thighs.

He wrapped one arm around her back, pulling her against him as he guided his rock-hard erection to her sweet, warm heat.

"Sit on my cock, baby," he urged, nuzzling her neck.

Kylie moaned softly, shifting her hips forward, spreading her knees wide so he could slide into the heaven of her body, never stopping what she was doing.

Travis groaned as her silky heat enveloped him, but it wasn't enough.

Needing to watch what she was doing, Travis repositioned his upper body, leaning into the cushion so he could watch as she wrapped her lips around Gage while she worked herself onto his cock. Gage's hand was fisting in Travis's hair, as though he needed to touch him.

Their ministrations were a feast for the eyes, perhaps more so than the unbelievable friction of her body as she sheathed him inside her. Not wanting to break her stride, Travis guided her hips, pushing deep inside her as he pulled her closer, retreating when he shifted her back. Travis looked up, watched the pleasure contort Gage's face as he fucked their wife's mouth with long, deep strokes.

Travis knew he would relive this moment for days because he always did. Whenever the three of them were together, didn't matter what they were doing, he thought about it endlessly, and it always ended the same. With him smiling, grateful for the life he'd been granted despite the obstacles they'd had to overcome.

Kylie's soft moans turned to insistent whimpers, her body vibrating. Travis worked his hands beneath the T-shirt, cupped her heavy breasts, causing those pleading mewls to increase.

"I'm gonna come in your mouth," Gage warned her, his voice raspy with need.

Kylie gave him a murmur of approval, her body rocking more intently.

Wanting to send her over at the same time, Travis gripped her hip with one hand, slid the other between their bodies, his thumb seeking her clit. When he pressed the tiny bundle of nerves, Kylie whimpered and moaned. And when he drove his hips upward, filling her completely, she panted, her mouth falling open.

Gage's fingers linked in her hair, holding her in place as he chased his release. Travis did the same, every muscle in his body coiling tightly as Kylie's pussy clamped down on him. He could feel her body vibrating, knew she was close.

Travis met Gage's eyes. The heat and love he saw there threatened to snap his control. He grunted as he slammed his hips up, back, up, back, holding Kylie in place so he could go deeper.

A feral growl sounded from Gage at the same time Kylie's pussy locked onto his cock, milking him as she came. Travis let himself go, his body shuddering as his release barreled through him.

When they were finished, Travis pulled Kylie down with him as he held up a hand, signaling Gage to join them.

As they had a million times over the years, Gage eased onto the couch, the three of them piled in a heap, too tired to move, too blissed out to care.

"Merry Christmas," he whispered with a smile.

Even as he accepted he was happier than he'd ever been, Travis couldn't help wondering how he could make their next Christmas even better than this one.

Sunday, December 29, 2019

MACK WALKED THROUGH HIS FRONT DOOR A little after three in the morning. He was exhausted, ready to fall into bed. He'd put in a full night at Moonshiners, dealing with the rowdy crowd pre-celebrating the coming of the new year.

He would have headed right for his bed if he could've gotten his mind to shut off. Instead, he snatched the open bottle of Jack Daniels he'd left on the kitchen table and detoured back to the living room, dropped onto the couch. Though the remote was in reach, he didn't bother to turn on the television. There wasn't anything that could distract his thoughts, so it wasn't worth the energy.

With Christmas over, the day-to-day grind back in full swing, Mack should've had enough to keep him busy. Even with New Year's looming in the not-so-distant future, he found there was nothing to look forward to.

He uncapped the whiskey, took a long pull on the bottle. After the liquid blazed fire down his throat and into his belly, Mack let his head fall back. He was inundated with memories of the night he'd spent with Jeff at the resort. More times than he could count, he'd picked up his cell phone, wanting to send the man a text, request his company, but every time, he'd backed out.

It was pointless, after all.

There was no happily ever after for Mack. Not with Jeff anyway.

Not anymore.

Unfortunately, Mack had made a promise to Daniel that he would consider what his son had proposed: sell the bar, move to Austin, spend more time with his son. While he loved Jeff, he was duty-bound to love his son more, so he knew he had to take the high road even if he had to forsake his own happiness to do so.

He groaned, lifting his head and downing more whiskey, desperate to dull the ache in his chest. Eventually he would numb out, though it would likely take the entire bottle. It took more these days, but he didn't mind drowning himself in the better part of a fifth of whiskey to accomplish his goal. After all, he had nothing better to do.

Mack was getting rather comfortable, his lips maintaining a steady connection with the bottle when his phone buzzed. He shifted, dragging it out of his back pocket, wondering how he hadn't broken the damn thing yet.

His vision was wavering as he glanced at the screen.

Jeff: *Unlock your front door.*

Mack stared at the phone, confused. He never locked his door, so why did he—

A soft rap sounded and he turned his attention to the wood as it opened.

When Jeff appeared, Mack couldn't even muster the energy to move.

He knew what he looked like. His beard was scraggly, hair likely sticking up all over the place. The fifth of Jack was balancing precariously on his thigh, his eyes likely bloodshot from a mixture of alcohol and exhaustion.

"You can't be here," Mack slurred, but didn't bother to move. He didn't have the energy.

Jeff stepped into the house, closed and locked the door behind him.

Mack glared at him. "You need to leave."

The sheriff looked like the officer of the law he was, all decked out in his brown-on-brown uniform. No one looked good in brown. Well, no one but Jeff. He looked good in anything. He looked better in nothing.

Fucking hell.

To his shock, Jeff began removing his clothes right there in Mack's living room, starting with his belt.

Mack stared, unable to look away, wondering if this was a dream. He sure as hell hoped so, because Jeff had no business being there. What if Daniel showed up? The kid did so from time to time, pretending he was just dropping by to check in when Mack knew it was more because he was keeping tabs, ensuring Mack wasn't doing anything he wasn't supposed to.

Which seemed to be anything that made him happy.

Mack grunted when Jeff removed the bottle from his hand, set it on the rickety end table beside the cheap brass lamp that Mack couldn't even remember buying but that had decorated the room for the past two decades.

He met and held the sheriff's hazel eyes, tempted to tell him to get the hell out, but the words wouldn't form in his mouth.

Oh, no. Mack was more of a glutton for punishment than he thought, because instead of standing his ground, he sat up, reached for the waistband on Jeff's pants, and tugged him closer.

Like Daniel told him, he was probably going to hell, but if that was the case, Mack intended to do so with a fucking smile on his face. After all, it wouldn't matter in the long run, because Mack knew he would end up letting his son dictate his actions. Could be a week, a month. Six. Eventually, he would sell the bar, say goodbye to his friends, and put this dusty little town in his rearview along with the sexy fucking sheriff who owned him heart, body, and soul.

But before that happened, he could indulge himself.

Yes, tonight he could indulge.

Tomorrow he could seek forgiveness.

Keep reading for the next in the Walker family saga.

Mack
(The Walkers of Coyote Ridge, 8)

Available now.

Prologue

Four years ago…

STARING AT HIS PHONE, MICHAEL "MACK" SCHWARTZ felt a cold chill slither down his spine. The kind caused by tragedy, loss, anything that resulted in emotional devastation.

Daniel: *We need to talk. Today.*

"Everything all right?"

Jerking his attention away from the cell, Mack looked up at Jeff, forced a smile. "Yeah. Of course."

Mack could see the doubt, the concern in Jeff's hazel eyes. It seemed to be there all the time now, and Mack wondered if he felt it, too. Something was about to happen, something that would change the course of their lives forever. Which, honestly, sucked major ass, because Mack was too damn old for this shit. Granted, age was merely a number, not a barometer. At fifty-two, he honestly felt as though he'd just started living his life.

With Jeff.

Only shit had gone awry a couple of months ago, back when Mack had stupidly inquired about Alluring Indulgence Resort. He'd been curious, no reason to deny it. And his curiosity had turned out to be the sparks that would soon burn his world to the ground. Since that night at the resort, rumors had begun to spread through Coyote Ridge, rumors claiming Mack and Jeff were together, something they'd done well to hide for the three years they'd been dating.

It wasn't that Mack gave a shit who knew, but he knew they had to keep it on the DL because Jeff was in the public eye, the sheriff of Coyote Ridge. It was an electable position, which meant Jeff had to appeal to the masses or he risked losing the career he'd worked so hard to establish. The thought of Jeff going down in those flames … it caused an ache Mack wasn't sure he could deal with.

"Well, I'll see you tonight," Jeff said softly, stepping toward him.

Mack knew he was waiting for a kiss, so he reluctantly offered one because sending him off into the dangers of his job without it was like telling the man he didn't care, and that couldn't be further from the truth.

After Jeff left for work, Mack locked up the man's house, got in his truck, and headed for Moonshiners. For the first time in a damn long time, he dreaded the thought of going into work. Not only because he knew he would garner a few stares since people were now curious as to what he was doing behind closed doors, but more so because he knew he would have to deal with Daniel. Anytime his son demanded they talk, it never ended well. For the past thirteen years, their relationship had been on rocky ground. Ever since Daniel learned that Mack was gay, a secret Daniel's mother had promised to keep. Not that Mack blamed her for telling the boy the truth. It wasn't her fault even if she'd gone about it the wrong way. In a perfect world, Mack would've been the one to tell him.

But they all knew the world wasn't perfect.

Not even close.

When Mack pulled into Moonshiners, the parking lot was empty as usual this early. He drove through the gravel lot and parked at the back, using the rear entrance to get inside. As he went through, flipping on the lights, his gut tightened into knots. He wanted to call Daniel, to tell the boy he didn't have time to talk tonight, but it would've been a lie, and Mack had made a point not to lie to the kid. Not ever again.

He made a detour into the small office he rarely used, unlocked the safe, and retrieved the cash box he kept inside. He transferred some of the bills to the register he kept beneath the bar, then turned on the credit card machine so it would be ready for the customers once they came in. He was about to head to the stockroom to unload yesterday's delivery when there was a pounding on the front door.

Dread made his stomach churn, but he forced his boots to carry him to the door. Using the key tethered to his belt loop, he unlocked the door, pushed it open. The glare of the setting sun backlit Daniel, casting his face in shadow as the boy stepped inside. Mack didn't need to see his face to know he was angry. It was etched into the tense lines of his shoulders, the clenched fists at his sides.

"Hey," Mack greeted softly, not bothering to lock the door behind him. He got the feeling Daniel wouldn't be staying long.

Daniel spun around to face him. "Why'd you do it?"

Mack stopped, met Daniel's blue stare. "Do what?"

"Make a mockery of yourself?"

The heat in his son's words threatened to singe Mack's beard, but he held his ground. "You'll need to be more specific."

"You think it's funny that the whole town thinks you're an abomination?"

Mack frowned, but his throat was too tight for any words to escape.

Daniel pivoted away from him, marched toward the bar only to stomp back toward him.

"I don't even live here and I'm up to speed on the fact that you're a laughingstock in this town. You and the sheriff, Dad? You just couldn't help yourself, could you? Couldn't simply keep that shit locked up tight. You had to go and let the world know."

Mack's shock turned to anger, but he held on to it. Daniel had every right to be angry with him.

"It ends now," Daniel demanded, his eyes blazing with hatred. "If you want a relationship with me, this bullshit with the sheriff ends now. Tonight."

Mack swallowed past the lump in his throat.

"You owe me this," Daniel insisted. "You lied to me growing up, then I had to hear it from my mother. She didn't bother to sugarcoat her thoughts on it, either, Dad. You're an abomination. Soiled and dirty and you used her."

Used her? Mack was confused. He'd never used Meredith. Granted, he'd done his best to love her, but he'd never been able to do it. Not because she wasn't worthy but because ... because Mack had always known deep down he couldn't love a woman. He wasn't built that way. And yes, he had failed her epically, but he'd done right by his son. Truth was, he loved Daniel more than he loved himself, and the only thing he'd ever wanted was for his son to be happy.

"If you don't end it with him, you'll never see me again," Daniel seethed.

"Daniel, please don't—"

"I mean it. End it with him so this town stops thinkin' you're some sort of deviant, Dad. You owe me that much."

Inhaling deeply, Mack tried to relax even as his heart constricted in his chest. If he didn't know better, he'd think he was having a heart attack. But this wasn't a cardiac event that could be detected on a machine. After all, broken hearts couldn't be seen on an X-ray or an MRI or whatever machine they used to check out that vital organ.

Daniel took a step closer, locked eyes with Mack. "Prove to me that I mean more to you than anyone else."

"Okay," he said softly.

Daniel's eyes narrowed. "You'll break it off with him?"

"Yes."

"Tonight. I don't want to find out you've spent another night with him, understand?"

Mack nodded.

"But don't think for a second this makes up for the hell you've put me through," Daniel said, his voice rough with his anger.

"I don't," he assured his boy. "And I'm sorry."

"You should be. But I promise, you'll be making this up to me for a long damn time."

It would be years before Mack truly understood how sincere Daniel was about that promise.

If you're interested in knowing more about Kaden, Keegan and Bristol, keep reading.

Kaden & Keegan
(The Walkers of Coyote Ridge, 9)

Available now.

Chapter One

KEEGAN WALKER STARED AT HIS TWIN, DOING his damnedest to get the man to come over to his way of thinking. Being as he'd been working on Kaden for the better part of ten minutes, it wasn't looking good for him.

"All right. What about a bakery?"

"Coyote Ridge already has a bakery," Kaden countered.

"Pet store?"

"No."

"Gym?"

"No."

"Vape shop?"

Kaden shot him a *get real* look. "No."

"Thrift shop?" Of course, that had Keegan doing his rendition of Macklemore's "Thrift Shop." "I'm gonna *pop* some *tags* … only got twenty *dollas* in my pocket."

A little too much twang, he thought, but not terrible.

"Stick to your day job, Keeg."

Yeah, yeah, yeah. Whatever. "Fine. No thrift shop. What about an arcade?"

Kaden narrowed his eyes in that manner that spoke of disbelief combined with a modicum of concern. "Seriously?"

"Yeah. Seriously." Keegan *was* serious, and he wasn't sure how much clearer he could be. Yet Kaden didn't seem to be on board, hence the reason he was feigning ignorance.

"Is this some sorta midlife crisis?" Kaden questioned, his dark eyebrow lowered at a sharp slant, his incredulity evident.

"First off, we're a long damn way from *midlife*. And two, it's a damn fine idea and you know it."

"Oh, yeah? And who in their right mind is gonna hang out in an arcade? In Coyote Ridge?"

"Just because *you're* old doesn't mean we all are," Keegan argued, staring at the man who was more or less his mirror image. "Have you seen the town lately? They're finally gettin' with the program."

"Yada, yada, I got it," Kaden sniped. "Ever since Rex opened the B and B, blah, blah. I know the spiel, Keeg."

But what a spiel it was. The Double R Bed and Breakfast had been open for a year, and it had proven to be a fruitful venture in just a short time. The big, renovated farmhouse right in the heart of town had been at capacity every weekend since the opening, and it didn't appear they'd be letting up anytime soon. What more could a small-town hotel ask for? Or those who had invested in the project from the jump?

Keegan grinned wide. "Damn good idea, wasn't it? I knew that place would be a helluva investment."

"Frog giggin', cow tippin', and a B and B. What more could Coyote Ridge *possibly* offer?" Kaden grumbled.

"An arcade," Keegan answered, deadpan.

Kaden rolled his eyes again.

Keegan had known his brother would react this way. They might share the same DNA code, but there was no denying their personalities were polar opposite. Kaden had always been the level-headed one, the one who came up with a plan even when a plan wasn't necessary. Keegan was more of the fly-by-the-seat-of-your-pants kinda guy. He tried not to take things too seriously, while Kaden spent more time thinking than actually doing. And sure, Keegan could admit his brother was usually right when it came down to their arguments.

Didn't mean Keegan agreed with his twin. In fact, most of the time they didn't see eye to eye at all.

But…

Yes, but. Backing Rex Sharpe in the bed-and-breakfast had been a stellar idea if he did say so himself. And now, who was to say an arcade couldn't bring some life to this sleepy little town? Of course, Keegan was only considering it because his true dream couldn't be realized yet. It had always been his goal to own a ranch, but without one available to acquire, that was unfortunately on the back burner.

"Well"—Keegan lifted his coffee mug, offered his brother a casual one-shoulder shrug—"I think it's a smart idea. Think about all the things Coyote Ridge has goin' for it. Just in the time we've been here, they've opened a toy store and a bookstore, right on Main Street. I heard they're plannin' to expand the bookstore to include a coffee shop. An arcade might kick it up a notch."

"I get my coffee at the bakery," Kaden retorted.

"*Options*, Kaden. We're always open for *options*."

"No. No way," Kaden retorted. "I'll admit, I doubted the B and B in the beginning, and it turned out all right, but I'm not at all on board with an arcade."

"Okay, fine," Keegan conceded. "What then? It's not set in stone and the place is still for sale. We can snatch it up, put in somethin' of our own." He leaned in, lowered his voice. "For fuck's sake, everyone else is doin' it. Why can't we?"

"If everyone else was jumpin' off a cliff, would you wanna do that, too, Keeg?"

He grinned. "Damn straight I would."

Those familiar steel-blue eyes glinted with incredulity. "You're serious? You want... *Us*? You and me...?" Kaden exhaled with a sigh and shook his head. "Ain't gonna happen, Keeg."

Keegan chuckled. He happened to enjoy getting his brother riled. Especially first thing in the morning.

"I'll come up with somethin'," he told his twin. "You just wait." Although he certainly wasn't giving up on the arcade.

Kaden challenged him back with a simple tilt of his eyebrows upward.

Keegan knew that look. Kaden thought he was off his rocker. And perhaps he was, but hey, everyone else seemed to be making their mark on this town. Why couldn't they?

Kaden leaned back, allowed the waitress to set his plate down in front of him. "Thanks." He turned his full attention to Keegan. "Might I remind you, we've got enough on our plates."

Keegan smiled at the waitress. "Thanks, doll." He peered over at his brother. "What? With Walker Demo? That's gonna be our claim to fame?" It was his turn to shake his head. "In case you didn't notice, it just kicked over leadership again."

Granted, that was because Reese Tavoularis had moved on to the governor's task force, another brainchild of their cousin Travis Walker. In Reese's place, Autumn Jameson—one of Travis's many cousins on his mother's side—had come on board to run things. She'd been in her new role for nearly a month, and to his surprise, she was doing pretty darn well. He was tempted to say she could pinpoint an issue with an engine faster than he could. But that didn't change the fact that even the family business didn't seem all that stable.

"What about the time we're puttin' in on the ranch?" Kaden asked.

"Key word there bein' *the*. *The* ranch infers that it doesn't belong to us."

As much as he enjoyed working on the Walker ranch, which belonged to Uncle Curtis and Aunt Lorrie, it had always been a dream of his to have one of his own. And yes, Keegan was keeping his eyes open for that opportunity. If it were to arise tomorrow, he'd drop every damn thing else and follow his dream. Until then...

Silence settled between them as Kaden covered his scrambled eggs in tabasco sauce. Rather than stir him up more, Keegan took a sip of his orange juice, stared at his pancakes. He always had pancakes. Every damn day. Why? At what point in his thirty-seven years had he gotten so damn … boring?

"Are you really serious about this? Openin' a place of our own?" Kaden finally asked, his voice lowered.

"Hell, I don't know. I'm just…" He met his twin's eyes. "I'm tired of watchin' everyone else doin' their thing while we settle for bein' along for the ride."

Kaden sighed.

Keegan sat up straight, picked up his fork. "Tell you what. I'm gonna stuff my face with these pancakes and we can pretend this conversation never happened. Deal?"

Kaden's blue-gray eyes locked on his face, but Keegan didn't flinch. He knew how he sounded. Petulant, whiny, sullen. Take your pick.

In his defense, Keegan had always allowed Kaden to make the final decisions. Sure, he threw in his two cents, like where they were gonna put down roots. His choice had always been Coyote Ridge, and since they were metaphorically attached at the hip, where one of them went, the other followed. When they arrived here, they'd thought it would be a fruitful venture. Years later, although they'd technically settled in, they weren't completely settled.

"Fine," Kaden huffed, grabbing his coffee mug. "Let's talk to Travis. Get his thoughts."

Great. Go to the man with the plan and tell him what? That they didn't have a plan? Yeah, no thank you. Their cousin Travis was not just *paving* the way here in Coyote Ridge, he *was* the way. Hell, after Travis's daughter was kidnapped a few weeks back, a task force governing the state of Texas had been formed to search for other missing people. Thank the good Lord, Kate had been located and returned seemingly unharmed two painfully long days after she went missing, but still. Guy had some serious pull. Not to mention, half the town went to Travis for advice. Keegan didn't want to be another in that long line.

Keegan sipped his juice, glared at his pancakes.

They finished their breakfast in silence, although it was obvious Kaden's mind was running a million miles a minute. That was the way his twin's brain worked. Whenever Keegan planted an idea, his brother would veto it immediately, then spend considerable time mulling it over until he came to a final decision. Generally, Keegan would go along with whatever his brother wanted, because truth was, Keegan was the laid-back one. Most things he could simply take or leave. Didn't matter. But something hadn't been sitting well with him lately.

While living and working in this small town had always been a dream of his, there was only one teeny tiny problem... They hadn't really put down roots. When Keegan took stock of what they had to call their own ... besides their trucks, there wasn't much of anything.

Take the house they occupied, for instance. Someone else's. Technically, it was now just one of seven separate structures Curtis had built for his boys when they were old enough to venture out on their own. Originally, it had been Kaleb's place. Then it was Jared's for a bit. Now it was theirs until they figured out what they wanted to do.

To buy or not to buy? Coyote Ridge or bust? For the moment, their options were open although real estate in Coyote Ridge was scarce and what did come available was usually snatched up within hours of being listed. If it ever made it to listing at all. Just like the building on Main Street. If they didn't make their play, it would be gone before they knew it. There wasn't even an apartment to be had. Not that Keegan had any desire to live in an apartment. He preferred wide-open spaces.

Sure, he loved Coyote Ridge. Had since he was a kid, when their parents would bring them and their brothers and sister down to visit their aunts and uncles. He remembered one summer—they were probably twelve, maybe thirteen—his brothers and sister all ganged up on their parents, tried to convince them to move to the small town their father had grown up in. Their parents won in the end, determined to hold down the fort in El Paso, but they'd all talked about moving here eventually.

Their oldest brother was the first to take the leap, relocating to Coyote Ridge permanently. Jared had fled a bad situation only to have it all turn around for the best once he settled down here. Of course, Quinn and Eve had rolled in only a month ago, with Wesley promising to pull up the rear sometime in the next year. At the very least, Wesley had promised to make it down here at some point during the holidays. Keegan was looking forward to seeing their overachieving doctor brother as well as their parents.

Even having his family close wasn't doing what it used to though. Keegan wanted something more.

Then again, perhaps that didn't have anything to do with the house they lived in or the jobs they held or the hobbies they'd picked up along the way. In most ways, they had the life they'd hoped for. Perhaps his settling-down issue had more to do with a some*one*, not necessarily a some*thing*.

That, of course, was Kaden's fault. His twin was still adamant they would eventually have the big wedding and greet some sweet young thing at the end of the aisle where they would vow to love endlessly, blah, blah, fucking blah. Keegan was no longer disillusioned in that area. Been there, done that. Twice. Another ride on the merry-go-round that was shitty relationships? No fucking thank you.

Unfortunately, he was starting to suspect Kaden had a specific woman in mind.

Did he still want to share women with his twin? Damn straight. He didn't know any other way. Their desire to share women between them was something that had come naturally since they were old enough to don a condom. Then it had been sealed thanks to Mrs. Whitley, the sexy housewife who'd turned two horny teenagers into men. Some found their untraditional need an abomination, but that had always been the way it was for them, and Keegan wasn't the sort to make excuses for it.

It was the marriage part he wasn't on board with. Nothing permanent, either. Fucking for the sake of fucking, that was his motto. Why, you ask? Well, that was because their attempts at happily ever after had blown up in their faces not once but twice in their history. Thank the good Lord, they'd never made it to the altar either time, but that had been the plan.

He was still on board with shagging the same chick, but he was no longer interested in seeing if it would lead to something more. It wouldn't. Might as well steer clear of the heartache.

Which was another reason Keegan was content to live in Coyote Ridge. He saw the way people treated Travis, Kylie, and Gage. They certainly weren't abominations and they were making the ménage à trois work. Of course, that was a different version of what Keegan and Kaden engaged in. Travis was in love with both Kylie and Gage, he was intimate with both of them, while Keegan and Kaden merely wanted to bang a willing, sexy woman from both ends. At the same time.

Crude, yeah, he could see that.

And yes, he was jaded.

So fucking what.

Kaden's cell phone rang, drawing Keegan from his rambling thoughts.

His brother snatched the phone off the table. "What's up, Trav?"

Keegan watched Kaden's face, waited to see what emergency they were being dragged into now. For whatever reason, they were the go-tos when it came to helping out Curtis's branch of the Walker family tree.

"Absolutely. We can run by there now, take them to the daycare. No problem."

Keegan grinned. Looked as though they were on chauffeur duty again.

When Kaden hung up, he grabbed his napkin, wiped his mouth, and signaled the waitress over.

"What was that about?"

Kaden reviewed the check, pulled out some cash. "Travis needs us to run by his house and pick up Kade, Avery, and Maddox. Asked us to drop them off at the daycare."

"Somethin' wrong?"

Kaden got to his feet. "Said Haden isn't feelin' well. Runnin' a fever. Kylie's hesitant to get him outta the house."

"Can't blame her there. What about Kate? She back at school yet?" Keegan asked, hopeful the little darling was finding some normalcy again after her horrific ordeal with the crazy psycho bitch who'd snatched her.

"Not yet. Travis said she's with him at the resort. Gonna take her to Lorrie this afternoon."

Keegan got to his feet, grabbed a five out of his wallet, and tossed it onto the table along with the money his brother left.

"I covered the tip already," Kaden mumbled as they were walking toward the door.

"And I bumped it a little. Now she'll be happy to see us next time we come in."

Kaden smirked. "She's happy to see us already."

Yeah, but Keegan was still on the fence as to whether he was going to attempt to get her phone number or not. Never hurt to be extra nice.

You know, just in case.

HALF AN HOUR LATER, KADEN WAS HOPPING out of the truck while his brother carried on a conversation with the three kids strapped into their car seats in the back seat. Kaden couldn't help it, he was laughing at some ridiculous joke Keegan told. Didn't matter that it was juvenile and rather simple, he still laughed.

Kaden had to admit, he was a tad jealous of how easily Keegan got along with the little ones. His twin was the guy all the kids wanted to be around, the one they chased over and under the jungle gym, shot with water guns on Sunday afternoons, hunted Easter eggs with, opened presents with. In recent months, Keegan had even claimed Beau's title belt as the favorite uncle, although technically they were cousins, not uncles.

Granted, that transition only happened because Beau was ear-deep in dirty diapers of his own with the rowdy triplets. Beau had promised Keegan he would be back to challenge him for the title, but he needed some time to settle in. Kaden had to wonder how true that was because the triple terrors were now one, and Beau was still on hiatus, his return to glory still iffy.

Didn't seem to bother Keegan in the least. In fact, Kaden was pretty sure Keegan was mighty proud of the title.

Funny thing was, Keegan didn't have to try too hard to be the favorite. He was merely good with kids. Kaden, on the other hand, loved the little munchkins, but he didn't have the smooth way that Keegan did. His brother would talk them into damn near anything, including brushing their teeth and eating their vegetables. The guy was a miracle worker.

At one point, Kaden had figured they'd have a houseful of their own rugrats by now, a ranch to raise them on. Some sweet woman sleeping between them, waking them up with a smile, a woman they could love beyond reason, spoil because she deserved it. So far, it hadn't happened, but he hadn't lost faith.

Kaden even had one particular woman in mind, but he found himself trying to navigate a couple of obstacles.

One: Bristol Newton, the sassy daycare owner he'd set his eye on, was proving to be resistant to their charms. A problem Kaden figured could be remedied if he just put his heart into it.

Two: Keegan. His twin was adamantly opposed to happily ever after. According to him, it wasn't possible, so why bother. He did, however, say *just sex* was always on the table.

Kaden didn't really see Bristol as the *just-sex* kinda girl, which brought him around to those obstacles he was still attempting to hurdle.

"Man, y'all are lucky," Keegan was saying when Kaden opened the truck door to help Avery out of her car seat.

"Why? Why are we lucky, Uncle Keeg?" four-year-old Kade asked, smiling widely as Keegan leaned in on the other side of the truck to assist him out.

"Because y'all get to come here," Keegan explained, motioning toward the daycare.

And see Bristol. Kaden kept that thought to himself as he set Avery on her feet because, at three, the little girl was already too independent to be carried.

Kaden took her hand before shutting the rear door. When he reached the front of the truck, Keegan was joining him, one hand firmly held in Kade's, the other arm filled with eighteen-month-old Maddox.

"There's all kinds of cool stuff to play with here," Keegan continued.

Kaden grinned. It was pretty much the same conversation they had anytime they brought one of the kids here. There were currently twenty-three little ones between Curtis and Lorrie's seven sons, the last of the herd—Zane and V's Dustin—born last December. For the first time in years, none of the women were pregnant. And due to being far outnumbered by the short-legged Walkers, Kaden and Keegan were often called in to help out in one capacity or another.

As for the daycare, they'd brought almost all of them here at some point. Keegan had mastered the art of hyping them up to want to go in. On occasion, one would make a mad dash for the door in an attempt to escape, but by the time Kaden was leaving, the kids were always excited. That was Keegan for you.

"There is," Kade assured Keegan with a huge grin. "All *kinds* of stuff."

"That's just not fair," Keegan said as he opened the outer door, allowing Kade and Avery to step in before him, then Kaden. "I wanna play with the cool stuff."

Once inside, they remained in the small vestibule, waiting for the interior doors to be unlocked. No one was allowed in who wasn't on the approved list of visitors, had their fingerprints on file, and knew their specialized code. No exceptions.

Kaden stepped up to the keypad, typed in the six-digit code, pressed his finger to the scanner, and waited.

"Maybe Miss Bristol'll let you play, too," Kade told Keegan, his brow furrowed as he peered up, the spitting image of Travis only in miniature form. "I can ask her."

Keegan's response was a conspiratorial grin and a quick nod.

Kaden chuckled. God, he loved these kids. They were so damn innocent, reminding him of a simpler time. And he felt blessed to have a chance to hang out with his cousins and their little ones on a daily basis. Plus, from time to time, he got to hang with his brother Jared, spend some quality time with his own nephew and niece.

"You do that," Keegan told Kade. "If Miss Bristol says it's cool, maybe we can play for a few minutes."

On more than one occasion, Kaden had had to sit back and watch Keegan build block castles with the little kids. Sometimes he wondered if his twin wouldn't mind spending his day here just so he could do that.

The lock disengaged, allowing them to open the interior door. The instant Kade stepped inside, he released Keegan's hand and began jumping up and down. "Miss Bristol! Miss Bristol!" he squealed.

Bristol Newton peered up from her spot at the desk, her light blue eyes glittering, a smile tilting the corners of her full lips. Clearly Kade knew to wait until he was acknowledged.

She turned in her chair, giving Kade her full attention as she rested her elbows on her knees, leaning toward him. "Good mornin', Kade."

God, he loved that soft twang, the raspy sound of her voice.

Hi, Miss Bristol." Based on the puff of his cheeks, Kade was trying to stifle his energy, but his hands couldn't seem to remain still.

Bristol peered up at them, then back to Kade. She stood and stepped around the desk. "What has you so excited this mornin'?"

"Uncle Keegan wants to play with the cool stuff. Can he? Just for a little while? Purty please?"

While Bristol chatted it up with the kids, Kaden took a minute to admire her. From her shoulder-length brown hair pulled back in a sleek ponytail, to the pink Converse on her feet. She looked all of sixteen, although Kaden knew she'd hit the big three-one earlier in the year. He'd even been invited to the shindig. Of course, he'd come up with an excuse as to why he couldn't go. In his defense, Bristol had been dating some jackass at the time—a temporary thing that had lasted all of two weeks—and he hadn't been keen on subjecting himself to seeing her with another man.

127

In fact, ever since their incident at Alluring Indulgence last December, it seemed Bristol was attempting to keep them at a distance by flaunting other men. Didn't matter that they never lasted much past a first date and she never shared any stories of hope for something more with the many women in her orbit. If she had, perhaps he would've had to intervene. Since she seemed to be doing what she could to push him and his brother away, he'd been biding his time.

But she was single now.

Very single.

When those glittering eyes lifted to meet his, a wide grin on her face, he was hard-pressed to keep from winking at her, a bad habit he'd acquired when picking up women. Fortunately, he knew better. Bristol was not the sort of woman who would be impressed by a wink and a smile. She was far too smart for that. In fact, she'd rebuked every attempt he'd made to flirt with her in the past. Except for that one alcohol-fueled night. Still, that hadn't deterred him in the least. Of course, he'd thought for sure they'd made inroads with her last Christmas, but he should've known better.

"Well, all right," she told Kade with a chuckle before peering up at Keegan. "I think it'll be fine if Uncle Keegan hangs out for a bit."

"Yay!" Kade squealed, jumping up and down as he grabbed Keegan's hand and jerked him toward the door leading to the inner sanctum.

"Hold up, speedy. Your sister's gonna wanna join us."

Kaden remained in the front office as Keegan keyed his passcode in a secondary keypad and then motioned Avery in front of him, making the little girl giggle as Kade grabbed Avery's hand and took off at a trot toward the back the instant the door opened.

"Sometimes I think you should charge him for bein' here," Kaden told Bristol as he stepped over to the wide window that overlooked the room where the kids congregated, watching his brother pass Maddox off to a waiting teacher.

"I think it's sweet," she said, bending over to jot something down in her notebook before standing tall once more.

The outfit she wore was more for comfort than fashion, he figured, but the woman would've looked damn fine wearing a potato sack. The light blue skinny jeans couldn't have been more formfitting if they'd been painted on. The plus was how they showcased toned legs and a sinful ass while the oversized cream-colored sweatshirt hid the nice curves he knew she rocked on that petite frame.

Truth was, Kaden was usually drawn to leggy women, the ones who were closer to his six foot two inches. Bristol couldn't have been but a few inches over five feet. Still there was something about her that did it for him.

"I'll be sure to tell him you said that." Kaden grinned. "He likes when women call him sweet."

Speaking of sweet, Bristol was sweet enough to cause a toothache and sassy enough to square a man's shoulders. Not to mention, she was as stubborn as she was beautiful. Oddly enough, he didn't even have to wink to make Bristol blush. Despite the fact they'd spent countless hours in her presence, usually at one Walker function or another, he always detected a hint of nerves when she was around them.

"So, will you be attendin' the fall festival?" she asked while they stood watching as a group of kids built a block fort around Keegan.

Fall festival? They'd just had the back to school festival, hadn't they? He did a mental calculation, realized the fall festival was only a few days away. Next weekend, in fact.

"Is it just me or does Coyote Ridge have a festival for everything?"

Bristol smiled up at him, a flash of those pretty white teeth. "I think the mayor's responsible for that."

"It hasn't always been that way?"

"Oh, no." She shook her head. "Not like this, anyway. We've had one or two a year, but only for the past couple of years has it ramped up. It's kinda nice."

Nice wasn't the word he would've used. Saying there was a festival for everything wasn't an exaggeration. Just in the past year, he'd been suckered into attending a Valentine's festival, Founder's Day festival, Easter, Memorial Day, the Kick Off to Summer festival, July Fourth, Back to School, some kind of Ode to Pets festival, and now the town's long-running annual fall festival.

How exactly did anyone get anything done around this place when they spent so much damn time decorating and organizing events?

"I think it's her way of revitalizin' the town," Bristol continued. "Mayor Stewart is all about bringin' the residents together."

Kaden found himself mesmerized by Bristol's glossy pink lips and the twinkle in her eyes. He wanted to kiss those lips again, to slide his tongue along the seam and dip inside, hear her reaction. It had been too damn long since he'd gotten a taste of her.

"Does that mean you'll be attendin'?" he asked, breaking the hold she had over him and forcing his eyes to meet hers.

Bristol grinned. "Of course. Mayor Stewart roped me into it."

"I find it amusin' you refer to her as Mayor Stewart considerin' Bianca's your best friend."

Bristol laughed. "One of them, yes. But I do it because it irritates her."

That made him smile. He liked her sassiness. Kaden only wished she'd turn all that attitude on him sometime.

"Well?" she asked, still staring at him.

Kaden frowned. "Well, what?"

"Can I add you to the list of people attendin'?"

"Depends."

"On?"

Kaden held her stare and offered his best smile. "What's in it for me?"

Check out a sample of

REX
The Walkers of Coyote Ridge, 6

Available now!

Prologue

"I'M SERIOUS, RAFE. I'M GONNA DO IT," Rex Sharpe declared. "I'm gonna turn this place into a bed-and-breakfast. A big one. Fancy, too. People are gonna come from all over just to hang out here." He smirked. "And they won't wanna leave."

In less than a month, Rex would be seventeen, and he already knew *exactly* what he wanted to do with the rest of his life. It all revolved around this place, the old, eight-thousand-plus-square-foot farmhouse that sat right in the middle of town surrounded by the land his family had owned for generations. The same eight-thousand-plus-square-foot farmhouse that was practically falling down around them because their old man was a drunk and an asshole.

But if Rex had anything at all, it was hope. So much he floated on it these days, his dreams so close he could practically taste them.

"Whatever," his kid brother said with a dismissive sigh. "You can't do that. Dad ain't gonna let you. He said he's gonna sell it."

"The hell he is," Rex snarled. On the day Rex turned eighteen, it would all belong to him and his brother. That would be the day Rex could throw the old man off their property and do right by their heritage.

"I heard him tellin' Jolene he's gonna make a bundle," Rafe insisted, his gaze locked on the floor as he flipped the broken sole of his boot open and closed.

Rex wasn't going to argue with Rafe. Billy Don Sharpe was out of his mind if he thought he would do anything of the kind. No way would Rex allow that crazy old fucker to sell what rightfully belonged to him and Rafe. The old man didn't have any rights to it since Billy Don's own father had ensured it wouldn't end up in his hands. Chester Sharpe had shown Rex the will, which stated the land and everything on it belonged to Rex and Rafe should something happen to him.

That meant Billy Don just got to stay there for one more year. If Rex had a say in the matter, the mean old bastard wouldn't even get that.

"It's gonna happen, Rafe. I promise." Rex peeked out of the old shack they'd started using as a hideout from their father. At one time it had been a tool shed, but his old man had long ago hocked all the tools to buy beer. "He ain't gonna stop me. One more year, Rafe. That's all we gotta wait."

"You ain't seventeen yet," Rafe corrected, sounding like the twelve-year-old he was.

"I will be in twenty-three days."

"That feels like forever, Rex," Rafe grumbled. "For-ev-er."

Still very much a kid, Rafe thought a week was forever, but Rex understood what he meant. Sometimes a week did feel like a lifetime around here. But a year ... They could hold out for that long. They had to.

"It'll be here before you know it," he assured Rafe. "Just have to be patient."

The wind rattled the old boards of the shed as they sat silently for a minute.

"Well, I wanna help," Rafe finally said, his brown eyes widening. "Will ya let me help, Rex? Maybe I can handle the horses. You can do all the rest."

Rex chuckled as he sat back down on the dusty wood floor and glanced at his brother. "We're gonna have people to help us. Lots of people. They'll work here. In the house and in the barn. We'll pay 'em good, treat 'em nice so they stick around."

Unlike their daddy, who ran off everybody. Including all of Mama's family. Rex and Rafe had loved the rare chances they got to spend with their aunts and uncles, but Billy Don had seen to it that Mama wasn't allowed to associate with them anymore. Hell, even the teachers at Rex's school didn't want to deal with Billy Don.

"Like that place Mama took us to?" Rafe asked, his eyes wide with wonder, his voice quieter than usual. "That big ol' cowboy place with the swimmin' pool and the hay rides?"

"It was a lodge," Rex told him.

"It looked like a log cabin to me. Will it look like that? Can we make it look like that, Rex?"

Rex considered it for a moment, grinned. "Sure. Just like that. We'll rebuild the house, make it nice. Lots of rooms for people to stay. Put in a pool and a hot tub. We'll get a barn, some horses."

"And chickens? I wanna get some chickens."

"Fine. We'll get chickens, too."

Rafe stared at him for a moment as though considering something. When he spoke, his eyebrows lifted slowly. "Only one problem, Rex."

Rex narrowed his gaze, waited for Rafe to clarify.

"You don't know how to build a house."

Rex chuckled. "I'll learn. When I graduate, I'll find someone to teach me. Then I'll be able to do all the work by myself."

"Me, too. You said I could help."

"You will." Rex would make sure his kid brother got to help.

Rafe's gaze dropped to the floor, his shoulders hunching forward as he continued to pick at the toe of his boot. "I wish Mama was here. I miss her, Rex."

That familiar pain jolted through his chest. Rex missed her, too. Just thinking about Mama made his heart hurt, the ache still too fresh.

"I wish he was in jail," Rafe hissed. "That's where he belongs."

Rex could only nod in agreement.

According to the police reports, Mama had died from a head injury when she'd fallen down the stairs. According to Billy Don, Adele had been drinking. Rex knew better. On both counts. Adele had a glass of wine on occasion, but even that had been rare. And Rex knew she hadn't fallen down the stairs. Billy Don had more than likely hit her. Hard. Like he always did.

Unfortunately, Rex hadn't been there when it happened, and the sheriff wouldn't listen when Rex tried to tell him to look into it further. He acted like Rex didn't know anything. Didn't help that Sheriff Carl Monroe was one of Billy Don's oldest friends. If only Jeff Endsley, the deputy, had been there. Then perhaps someone might've done something.

They'd laid Mama to rest just nine months ago, one week after Christmas and only two months after their grandfather had passed away from a heart attack. Rex figured Billy Don had something to do with that, too, but he couldn't prove it. Billy Don had hated Grandpa. They were always arguing. Billy Don was the one yelling, cursing, saying horrible things about Mama right to Grandpa's face. Grandpa had defended Adele every chance he could, but as it turned out, not even Grandpa could put Billy Don in his place.

And now Rex and Rafe were on their own, stuck with Billy Don until Rex turned eighteen. The only two people Billy Don hadn't chased off were now six feet under.

Rex's ears perked up when he heard the back screen door slam. Rafe instinctively scooted farther against the wall, tucking his knees in close to his chest, making himself small.

"Rex! Where ya at, you little fucker?" Billy Don let out a sharp whistle. "Get yer ass in the house. Dinner ain't gonna cook itself."

Rex frowned. He'd been hoping the old man had passed out. Between the whiskey, the beer, and whatever he shot into his arm, it happened more often than not. Evidently, they wouldn't get that lucky tonight.

"You stay here for ten minutes, then come up to the porch." Rex squeezed Rafe's shoulder gently. "Make sure there ain't no yellin' before you come inside."

Rafe shook his head. "I wanna go with you."

"Lemme see how his mood is first," he warned his brother. "If he's swingin' fists, I don't want you in the house."

Billy Don was always itching for a fight, always beating on someone or something. It was the very reason they didn't have a dog anymore. When Rex had witnessed Billy Don kick the dog hard enough to send him sprawling across the room, Rex had lost it. He'd ended up with a black eye and a split lip when he lit into Billy Don, but Rex had somehow managed to deflect Billy Don's rage. They'd only had Rascal for two weeks when Rex had begged Grandpa to take him, to give him to someone who wouldn't hurt him. Grandpa had done it, even though Rafe had cried. Sure, Rex had felt bad for his brother, but not bad enough to change the outcome.

Most of the time, when Mama was alive, she'd been the one who dealt with the backhanded blows, the punches, and the nasty words. No matter how many times Rex tried to intervene, to stop the old man from hitting her, it only made things worse. At that point, Billy Don would hit her harder. Right up until that asshole killed her.

Now that Mama was gone, Rex was trying to keep the old man's focus on him. Being that Rafe was four years younger, it pained Rex to see his kid brother getting hit. If he could stop it, even if it meant taking the blows himself, then by God, he would.

"Don't let him hit you, Rex," Rafe whispered.

Rex pushed to his feet. "It'll be fine." He put his hand on the door and peeked out to ensure his old man wasn't still out there. "Ten minutes. If you hear yellin' inside, don't come in. Just come back here. I'll let you know when it's all right."

Rafe's eyes were wide, but he nodded his head, his mess of dark hair flopping over his forehead. Rex knew the kid wouldn't listen. He was hardheaded, a trait that seemed to run in their family.

Once he confirmed the coast was clear, Rex slipped out of the rickety shack and raced toward the back porch that was in worse condition than the tool shed. As usual, Rex's gaze scanned the huge farmhouse as he neared it. One day this place would belong to him and Rafe and they'd turn it into something nice, something worthy of their grandfather's legacy, a place everyone wanted to come. And Billy Don wouldn't be allowed anywhere near it.

Rex opened the screen door and stepped inside. Before his eyes could adjust to the dim interior, he was knocked forward, his father's big hand smacking him upside the head, making him stumble.

"Where you been, boy? I hollered ten minutes ago."

Rex's fists clenched at his sides, but he bit back the anger. It was getting harder and harder not to hit the old bastard. But he knew if he did, they'd likely cart his ass to jail and no one would be there to protect Rafe.

"I told you to get yer queer ass in here," Billy Don hissed.

Rex blanched just like he did every time his father said that. He wasn't sure if Billy Don actually knew that Rex found himself attracted to guys rather than girls or if he just got off on being crass. It turned his stomach all the same.

"I'm here," Rex said, putting distance between him and the drunk old man. Billy Don smelled like he hadn't showered in a week.

"Where's that snot-nosed brother of yours?"

Rex shrugged.

The old man turned to look out the screen door.

Knowing his father would go looking for Rafe simply because he wanted someone else to knock around, Rex figured he had to distract him.

"What'd'ya want for dinner?" Rex asked, heading to the sink to wash his hands. "I'm not sure what we've got. You ain't been to the store in a while."

"We got spaghetti, don't we?"

"Yeah." Besides the makings for PB and J, it was the only thing they ever had in the house.

Rex

"Then make it," his father ordered, turning around to face
him. He had a beer in one hand, a cigarette in the other. "Jo's
comin' over. You make sure there's enough for her."

Rex inwardly cringed at the mention of his father's girlfriend.
He absolutely hated Jolene Snyder. Not only because she'd been
coming around ever since their mama died, but also because she
creeped him out. Always trying to get close, sitting beside him,
putting her hand on his leg. When he tried to get away, she would
whine to his old man until Rex was forced to sit there and endure
it.

"You have a problem with that, boy?"

"No, sir." He kept his eyes down so his old man wouldn't see
the hatred he felt for him.

"Good. 'Cause tonight, I'm gonna let Jo talk to you 'bout a
few things." He sneered at Rex. "Said she's got a plan."

Rex frowned. He'd rather let his father beat on him than have
to talk to Jolene.

Thankfully, the old man disappeared into the living room.
Rex started the water to boil on the stove, then motioned Rafe into
the house when his brother appeared in the doorway.

"Jolene's comin' over," Rex whispered. "You're gonna have to
stay outta sight tonight."

All the color drained from Rafe's face. Rex got the feeling
Jolene had managed to corner his brother at least once, but
possibly more. He didn't want to think about what that vile woman
had done to Rafe, either. While Rex did his best to stand between
Rafe and the adults Billy Don brought around, he couldn't always
be there.

"I don't wanna stay here," Rafe insisted, his voice a rough,
high-pitched whisper. "I don't wanna see Jolene. Don't make me,
Rex. Please don't make me."

"I know." Rex pulled the spaghetti box out of the pantry, went
to work getting the pasta started. "I don't, either, but we ain't got
no choice. We ain't got nowhere else to go."

"What about Mama's brothers or sisters? Did you call them
yet?"

"Haven't had a chance," he said, although it wasn't exactly the truth. While he wished they could do something about Billy Don, Rex wasn't that naive. The last time he'd seen any of his family had been at their mother's funeral. Aunt Lorrie had told them to call if they ever needed anything, but Rex wasn't sure she knew what she would be getting herself into if he did.

So he was putting it off.

"Bring me another beer, boy!"

Rex shot a glare in the direction of his father's voice. He hated that old man. Hated everything about him, but most importantly, he hated that their father didn't give a shit about his own kids.

Not wanting Billy Don to come into the kitchen again, Rex hurried to grab a beer out of the fridge. He popped the top, delivered it to his father, then returned to the kitchen to find Rafe sitting on the floor, his knees up to his chest, back against the wall, gently rocking himself.

"I ain't gonna let them hurt you," Rex whispered, making noise with the pans to cover up the sound. "I swear it, Rafe."

His brother's dark brown eyes lifted, and Rex could see the fear and something that looked a lot like shame. "I hate her, Rex. Hate her so much."

"Me, too," Rex assured him. "But don't you worry 'bout nothin'. I got it all under control."

While the noodles boiled in the water, Rex made peanut butter and jelly sandwiches. It took five minutes for Rafe to scarf down one, along with a full glass of milk. Rex made quick work of two while he nuked a bowl of spaghetti sauce in the microwave.

"Go on up to your room," Rex whispered to Rafe when he was done. "Read a book or somethin' till I can finish up down here."

"Promise not to leave?" Rafe asked, his eyes pleading. "You're not gonna go see Bristol, are ya?"

"I swear it. I ain't goin' nowhere tonight." Rex mussed Rafe's hair, nudged him toward the back stairs. "Now, go."

Once Rafe was out of sight, Rex made his father a plate, delivered it to him before returning to the kitchen to clean up the mess he'd made.

He was a few minutes shy of being finished when the shrill whine of Jolene's car signaled her arrival.

Rex peered out the small window above the sink as the little silver Toyota bumped down the driveway, coming to a stop right outside the door. His teeth clamped together, anger filling him at the sight of Jolene driving their mama's car. When Mama died, Billy Don had given the car to Jolene as a present rather than let Rex have it like he should have. Rex had already learned how to drive, even had his license thanks to his grandpa.

Of course, Billy Don said Jolene deserved the car for all she did around their place. Rex knew it was more of a payment for sex than anything else. He still didn't know why Jolene was hanging around Billy Don considering the twenty-seven-year age difference, but hey, it wasn't his place to care, either.

On the other hand, he did know why his old man kept *her* around. As soon as Billy Don had put the car keys in her hand, Jolene had dropped to her knees right there on the back porch, unzipped Billy Don's jeans… The instant Rex had realized what was going on, he'd raced upstairs wishing he could bleach his brain to forget what he'd seen.

Hurrying to dry the last of the dishes, Rex prayed she would finish her cigarette outside, giving him ample time to disappear upstairs. He tossed silverware into the drawer, slammed it shut, and was just about to turn when he heard the screen door squeak on its hinges. He grabbed the rag to wipe down the counters, got busy.

"Hey, handsome," Jolene said in that raspy tone he was sure wasn't natural. "Sure smells good in here. Whatcha makin'?"

Rex's shoulders tensed but he didn't turn around and he didn't speak.

"Did you save me some supper?"

Without a word, Rex motioned toward the plastic containers he'd set on the counter by the stove.

"Aww, ain't you sweet," she said, her voice far too close for comfort. "I knew you were thinkin' 'bout me."

As he wiped the counter with one hand, Rex hurried to put the last plate in the cabinet, tossed the dish rag in the sink, and turned to go.

"Where're you goin' in such a hurry, Rexi boy?" Jolene asked, plastering herself against him.

He fucking hated that nickname she'd given him. Almost as much as he hated the way she smelled. Like tobacco, cheap perfume, and sweat. A disturbing combination that made his stomach twist in a knot.

Rex eased around her, doing his best not to make eye contact. From the moment Billy Don had introduced him to Jolene, he'd felt there was something seriously off about her. Mentally.

She could've been pretty if it weren't for her frizzy, bleached-blond hair, her black-lined, bloodshot eyes, and her fire-engine-red lipstick that clashed with her yellow teeth. Never mind the fact the woman didn't know what real clothes were. She was always wearing short-shorts and a tank top, showing off far too much skin, including all the track marks that ran down her arms. No doubt she was an addict and it didn't do much for her appearance. For a woman who was only twenty-one, she sure looked a hell of a lot older than that.

"My father's been waitin' for you," Rex told her as he kept to the perimeter of the room, heading for the stairs.

Jolene grinned, one hand sliding over her breast. "I'm worth the wait. Where's Rafe?"

"He's not feelin' well."

"Oh, that poor baby." She flicked her cigarette ashes toward the bowl on the table. "I'll have to come up and check on him in a bit."

"He's fine," Rex told her. "I'm takin' care of him."

Jolene suddenly blocked his path out of the kitchen and Rex forced his gaze to hers. At sixteen, he was already six three, a good foot taller than Jolene. She didn't seem bothered by the fact that he towered over her. In fact, he was almost positive she liked that he did. Whenever he looked at her, she always batted her eyes and licked her lips. It grossed him out every single time.

"Always takin' care of everyone else, Rexi boy," she crooned, then flipped her hair over her shoulder. "You're all grown up. A man already." She smiled, flashed dingy teeth. "But don't you worry. That's why I'm here. You need someone to take care of *you*."

Rex's stomach threatened to revolt.

When she reached for him, he jerked back, his elbow hitting the wall. "I'm fine takin' care of myself."

Her smile lost its sweetness and matched the meanness he saw in her eyes. "I know you are, handsome. I know you are. But sometimes you don't get to make the rules. Your daddy says I'm in charge when I'm here, so you might wanna be nicer to me." Her gaze raked over him. "You wouldn't want me to put you over my knee, would you?"

Jolene's cackling laugh sent chills down his spine. She seemed far too interested in doing just that.

"No, ma'am," he said, his tone serious.

"That's too bad," she pouted. "Might be kinda fun."

Rex continued toward the stairs, not turning his back on her. He didn't trust the woman any more than he trusted his father.

Her eyes followed him, but thankfully she didn't say anything else. As soon as his foot hit the first step, Rex turned and bolted, his boots slapping against the wood. Loud enough his father hollered to tell him to keep it down.

Once he was safely upstairs, Rex made a beeline for Rafe's room. He found his brother sitting on the bed reading a book. "Come on. You're stayin' in my room tonight. Bring your book."

Rafe didn't argue. Not that Rex had expected him to.

"Can I sleep in the closet, Rex?"

"Yeah, sure. Grab a pillow and blanket."

Maybe if they were lucky, Jolene would get high and pass out right along with their old man. Otherwise, it was going to be a long night.

Unfortunately, that was the night that changed the rest of their lives.

ACKNOWLEDGMENTS

Of course, I have to thank my wonderfully patient husband who puts up with me every single day. If it wasn't for him and his belief that I could (and can) do this, I wouldn't be writing this today. He has been my backbone, my rock, the very reason I continue to believe in myself. I love you for that, babe.

I also have to thank my street team – Naughty (and nice) Girls – Your unwavering support is something I will never take for granted.

I can't forget my copyeditor, Amy at Blue Otter Editing. Thank goodness I've got you to catch all my punctuation, grammar, and tense errors.

Nicole Nation 2.0 for the constant support and love. You've been there for me from almost the beginning. This group of ladies has kept me going for so long, I'm not sure I'd know what to do without them.

And, of course, YOU, the reader. Your emails, messages, posts, comments, tweets… they mean more to me than you can imagine. I thrive on hearing from you, knowing that my characters and my stories have touched you in some way keeps me going. I've been known to shed a tear or two when reading an email because you simply bring so much joy to my life with your support. I thank you for that.

About Nicole Edwards

New York Times and *USA Today* bestselling author Nicole Edwards lives in the suburbs of Austin, Texas with her husband and their youngest of three children. The two older ones have flown the coup, while the youngest is in high school. When Nicole is not writing about sexy alpha males and sassy, independent women, she can often be found with a book in hand or attempting to keep the dogs happy. You can find her hanging out on social media and interacting with her readers - even when she's supposed to be writing.

Want to know what's coming next? Or how about see some fun stuff related to Nicole's books? You can find these, as well as tons of other stuff on Nicole's website. You can also find A Day in the Life blog posts, which are short stories about your favorite characters, as well as exclusive contests by joining Nicole Nation on Nicole's website. To join, simply click **Log In | Register** in the menu.

If you're interested in keeping up to date on any new releases and preorders, you can sign up for Nicole's notification newsletter. This only goes out when she's got important information to share.

Want a simple, fast way to get updates on new releases? Sign up for text messaging. If you are in the U.S. simply text NICOLE to 64600 or sign up on her website. She promises not to spam your phone. This is just her way of letting you know what's happening because Nicole knows you're busy, but if you're anything like her, you always have your phone on you.

CONNECT WITH NICOLE

Website: NicoleEdwardsAuthor.com

Facebook:	/Author.Nicole.Edwards
Instagram:	NicoleEdwardsAuthor
Twitter:	@NicoleEAuthor

By Nicole Edwards

ALLURING INDULGENCE
Kaleb
Zane
Travis
Holidays with the Walker Brothers
Ethan
Braydon
Sawyer
Brendon

THE WALKERS OF COYOTE RIDGE
Curtis
Jared
Hard to Hold
Hard to Handle
Beau
Rex
A Coyote Ridge Christmas
Mack
Kaden & Keegan

BRANTLEY WALKER: OFF THE BOOKS
All In
Without a Trace
Hide & Seek

AUSTIN ARROWS
Rush
Kaufman

CLUB DESTINY
Conviction
Temptation
Addicted
Seduction
Infatuation
Captivated
Devotion
Perception
Entrusted
Adored
Distraction

DEAD HEAT RANCH
Boots Optional
Betting on Grace
Overnight Love

DEVIL'S BEND
Chasing Dreams
Vanishing Dreams

MISPLACED HALOS
Protected in Darkness
Salvation in Darkness
Bound in Darkness

OFFICE INTRIGUE
Office Intrigue
Intrigued Out of the Office
Their Rebellious Submissive
Their Famous Dominant
Their Ruthless Sadist
Their Naughty Student
Their Fairy Princess

PIER 70
Reckless
Fearless
Speechless
Harmless
Clueless

SNIPER 1 SECURITY
Wait for Morning
Never Say Never
Tomorrow's Too Late

SOUTHERN BOY MAFIA/DEVIL'S PLAYGROUND
Beautifully Brutal
Without Regret
Beautifully Loyal
Without Restraint

STANDALONE NOVELS
Unhinged Trilogy
A Million Tiny Pieces
Inked on Paper
Bad Reputation
Bad Business

NAUGHTY HOLIDAY EDITIONS
2015
2016